You CAN Afford to Stay Home With Your Kids

A Step-by-Step Guide for Converting Your
Family From Two Incomes to One

By
Malia McCawley Wyckoff
and Mary Snyder

D1111854

CAREER PRESS

Franklin Lakes, NJ

YOU CAN AFFORD TO STAY HOME WITH YOUR KIDS
Cover design by Cheryl Finbow
Printed in the U.S.A. by Book-mart Press

To order this title, please call toll-free 1-800-CAREER-1 (NJ and Canada: 201-848-0310) to order using VISA or MasterCard, or for further information on books from Career Press.

The Career Press, Inc., 3 Tice Road, PO Box 687, Franklin Lakes, NJ 07417

Library of Congress Cataloging-in-Publication Data

Wyckoff, Malia McCawley.
   You can afford to stay home with your kids : a step-by-step guide
for converting your family from two incomes to one / by Malia
McCawley Wyckoff and Mary Snyder.
     p.   cm.
   ISBN 1-56414-408-9
   1. Home economics—Accounting. 2. Budgets, Personal. I. Snyder,
Mary, 1963-   . II. Title.
TX326.W94   1999
640'.42—dc21   99-24073
                                                    CIP

We dedicate this book to all the important people in our lives:
Vaughn, Tim, Charity, Camille, Riley, Paige, and Maggie

Acknowledgments

We would like to thank all the people at Career Press, who were willing to take a chance on a couple of unknowns. Also, warm thanks to our agent, Sheree Bykofsky, for believing in this project enough to take us on and eventually bring us a contract. Thanks to Janet Rosen, the calmest, most efficient person we've ever talked to on the phone, for answering all of our silly questions. We would also like to express our gratitude to all the moms (and dads) at home who shared views from the trenches and showed us that our successes as single-income families weren't just flukes.

—*The Authors*

My heartfelt thanks to my husband, Vaughn, whose love and support gives me the opportunity to pursue my dreams. Thank you, honey, for putting up with my bouts of the crazies. Thanks to my wonderful daughters, Charity and Paige, for reminding me why I wanted to write this book in the first place and for not complaining too much when I was stuck in front of the computer for hours on end. And to my sister Jennifer, thank you for reminding me why this book was important. To my dear friend Laura Bowden, thanks for taking that first writing class with me. Your unfailing support and love has been a great comfort in this pursuit. My deepest gratitude to my mom and dad, Mary and Fred Whitworth, for raising me to believe I could achieve any dream.

—*Mary Snyder*

Without the constant support—and, at times, tolerance—from my husband, I would never have been able to stay home with the kids in the first place, let alone get this book written. Thank you, Tim, for your love, and thanks especially for the freedom you've given me to begin carving out my own niche in the world. And to our children—Camille, Maggie, and Riley—thanks for being the smartest, most loving, and all-around best kids that any mom could have. Now that the book is done, you all can go back to playing on the computer. And finally, to my parents, Libby and Mac McCawley, thank you for teaching me to recognize what's really important. I'm sure at times you thought I wasn't listening, but somehow the lessons took hold anyway.

—*Malia McCawley Wyckoff*

Contents

Part Three: The Nitty-Gritty: Home Economics

Been There, Done That

You're a working parent. It's 5:25 p.m. and your client is still discussing the minutiae of your proposed pricing plan. Beginning to panic, you grasp for some way to wrap up this meeting without appearing unprofessional or, worse, insensitive to the client's concerns. But the fact is, somebody has to pick up your child from day care before six o'clock, and it's too late to catch your spouse. Finally, you manage to break up the meeting, but you feel uneasy about it as you fly out the door.

The day-care center is chaotic as you grab your child and try to locate her jacket, which should be with her backpack, but isn't. It's the only jacket that fits, so you can't leave without it! Finally, the jacket appears and you hurry your child, who is talking a mile a minute, into the car. Traffic is horrible, but you finally arrive home at 6:45 p.m. Thank goodness you didn't have to stop at the grocery store, because you now have exactly one hour and 15 minutes to make dinner, give your child a bath, and get her into bed by eight. Still wearing your business clothes, you start yanking things out of the refrigerator as your spouse tries to look through the mail, entertain your child, and tell you about his day. You groan as you suddenly remember that you have a breakfast meeting tomorrow, and you need that navy suit you forgot to pick up at the cleaners.

Sound familiar? Of course it does. Millions of families experience this kind of mayhem every day. The details may be different, but the chaos and the harried feeling have become the norm. Are we happy with it? Some of us are. Some of us haven't had time to even consider the question. Many of us, though, inherently know that there has to be a better way.

We know many working parents, both men and women, who would love to stay home and raise their families. We pursued this dream for five or six years. We were working until we could afford to quit. In the meantime, we enjoyed our jobs (usually), reveled in our successes, and earned our promotions. We were good, solid employees with bright career futures. But it was the struggle to make ends meet that kept us there. The years slipped by with astonishing speed. We found ourselves trapped in our jobs by the lifestyle that work seemed to require of us.

Who should read this book, anyway?

We wrote this book for several reasons. Once we left our jobs and were actually home, it didn't take long to realize we could have quit sooner, if only we had known how. Prior to quitting, we had both read money management books, books on how to cut expenses, and books on how to work from home. While the majority of these texts had excellent suggestions, none of them helped us put the entire picture together. We still couldn't envision the process from getting ready financially to making it work day-to-day without starving. We still thought of quitting as a distant dream. Finally, unable to take the daily grind anymore, we both ended up just quitting anyway. Though this didn't kill us, we now see that there is an easier, safer way.

After making the change in our own lives, we saw the need others may have for the information in this book. People we know are always asking us how we are managing to stay home. These parents know that we are middle-class women whose husbands are not making a fortune. We tell them that we are careful with money, creative about running a household, and ruthless with regard to our priorities. And, frankly, that's how we do it, period. The responses we hear are all variations on the same theme: "I wish I could afford to quit." Or, "Unfortunately, there is no way we could get by on just one salary." Wrong. The pathways are there for the taking.

We wrote this book because we know we are not the only ones who want to have the time and energy to raise and nurture our families. "Family Values" has become a popular term these days. These buzzwords come out of the mouths of politicians over and over again. Why? Because "a return to family values" is what political phrase-makers sense many Americans want. Unfortunately, our government can't give us family values. Values come from ourselves. We transfer them to our children with repetition over time. The catch is, it's far easier to get *your* values into *your* family if you're not stressed out and exhausted when you're with them, *and* if you're with them more than one or two multitasking hours each day.

If you are a working mother, for example, consider this information from the U.S. Census Bureau: In 1995, 55 percent of women ages 15 to 44 who had given birth in the previous year were in the labor force. This went up from 31 percent in 1976. If the woman was 30 to 44, and the birth was her first, the percentage rose to 77 percent.

These are revealing statistics, given the stress on us all to restore "Family Values." Times are changing, and today's households and our roles in them are changing, too. For example, maybe your family is planning to send *Dad* home full-time. This book will work for you, too. We've formatted it to serve as a step-by-step guide for going from a dual-income family to a single-income family with one parent at home full-time. We don't expect that every suggestion will be useful to every family's situation, but we have included many suggestions from which you can pick and choose, according to your specific situation. In fact, you will find this book useful if any one of the following statements describes you.

- ◆ You're looking for a way out of the two-income-no-time-for-anything-but-work grind.
- ◆ One of you wants to stay home and raise the kids, but you think you can't afford to lose the income.
- ◆ You want or need to lower your monthly expenses.
- ◆ You or your partner is facing possible job loss.
- ◆ You're looking for ways to make your current income go further.
- ◆ You want to quit your job to start a home-based business.

There's more than one way off a speeding train

We both decided to make the jump. One of us carefully researched and began a home-based business to bridge the financial gap between full-time corporate employee and stay-at-home mom. The other one of us—totally overwhelmed by it all—just jumped, figuring she would take a couple of months off, and then get a part-time job if necessary. We were frightened at first. Quitting a job when you know you can't make it on one salary is ridiculously risky, but we were desperate.

Our families both started cutting costs everywhere we could. After some trial and error, we found ourselves cutting costs we hadn't realized we had. While we both had an idea of what the monthly financial deficit should be, without our regular paychecks, neither of us was prepared for what happened. After a couple of months, making ends meet wasn't as difficult as we expected. Some months finances got a little hairy, but finances sometimes got that way when we were working, too.

We are not recommending that anyone simply resign tomorrow. We now know that there are ways for you to slow down and confront getting off the double-income train first. At the very least, you will have to determine the train's speed. After deducting the obvious costs of working (childcare, for example), how much is really left of that second income? How much of a shortfall is there between the primary wage earner's net income and your current monthly expenditure? Can you make it work by simply cutting back, or do you need to pay off some bills first? Where can you free up some cash flow to use toward paying off some debt quickly? You need to answer these questions before you know how soon you can jump, and still land on your feet.

In addition to addressing the decision to quit working, the first part of this book includes charts to give you the big financial picture, ways to re-examine the costs that you think you're stuck with, and plenty of practical advice on making it all work. It can be done, and it's probably easier than you think.

What will it be like when I get there?

The most bewildering surprises, especially when we first left the work force, were the emotional and personal upheavals. That first morning when we woke up and didn't have to go to the office, sparked off a brief honeymoon period for us. The sense of freedom was exhilarating. We played with the kids. We made "To-Do" lists of all the projects we'd been putting off for years. We dug out all those books we never had time to read before. We met our husbands at the door. We even had fabulous dinners ready and waiting on the table.

Those first few weeks were bliss. Then came a day when we actually started to miss work. Had we made a terrible mistake, we wondered? Surely it wasn't the job we were missing, but what was it? We had all those things we wanted so badly: plenty of attention to shower on our children, the energy to fully participate in our marriages, and vast chunks of time to accomplish almost anything. Still, something was missing.

The "something" turned out to be several things. We missed the adult interaction we had at work. Although we remembered the days when all we wanted was for everyone to get out of our office and leave us alone, now we would happily chat with anyone over the age of 11. Our girlfriends weren't available because they were all at work. When we did talk to them, they seemed different. Maybe they were jealous. Maybe they felt guilty because we were home and they were not. Or maybe we just didn't have as much in common with them as we thought.

We were also missing the less tangible things that a "real" job provides. Without an imposed daily structure, we weren't really sure which thing to do first. As a result, we didn't seem to be getting much done at all. We didn't feel entirely competent, either. After all, there was no training seminar for running a household. Without quotas, deadlines, and manuals, we felt aimless and lost. Our expectations of staying home were about 40 percent realistic and 60 percent June Cleaver. We just didn't consider that June had much more practice, better neighbors, and a television script! The second part of this book will help you prepare for a realistic transition and take you through those first weeks and months as you settle into your new routine.

The nitty-gritty

You may be saying to yourself, "I'm here, I'm happy, but I wish I'd paid attention in Home Economics." Face it: Martha Stewart may be one of our icons, but she's really rich and has a huge staff of trained professionals. Without a doubt, hand-gilt antique mirrors and gingerbread mansions are good things, but we, on the other hand, are primarily concerned with the basics. We need our homes to run smoothly and within a budget, while still maintaining an enjoyable lifestyle. The third part of this book is packed with practical information and tips on how to live well on a single income. We've included everything from inexpensive activities for the kids to affordable family vacations to a list of pantry staples. There are sections on food, home, clothing, recreation, and more. We've also included a list of books, organizations and other resources for at-home parents.

If the single-income life sounds right for your family, pull up a chair, roll up your sleeves, and get ready to change your life.

Part One

Tearing Yourself Away From the Two-Income Grind

Chapter 1

I Have It All, But I Want to Give Some of It Back

The reality of having it all

Can anyone really have it all? Well, most people can have *some* of it, but can anyone really have *all* of it? Besides, what does "having it all" really mean, anyway? In the 1970s, "having it all" for many of us meant having a fantastic, exciting career; a wonderful marriage to an understanding and sensitive spouse; happy, healthy, well-adjusted children; and gourmet dinners. In the 1980s, we added things to the dream list, such as a great house; a designer wardrobe (entirely black); family vacations to Club Med; $80 running shoes; a physically fit body (thanks to a personal trainer); stimulating conversation with fascinating friends; an enviable stock portfolio; and maybe even a dog. Is it any wonder that now we need self-help books and aromatherapy?

The reality of having it all is that most people *can't*—at least not the way we have it set up. There are only 24 hours in a day, and if you're chasing the elusive *all*, something is getting shortchanged. For us, that "something" was our family and ourselves. Our 40-hour-per-week jobs easily ate up 60 hours every week, and life's basics—dinner, laundry, grocery shopping, baths and showers, sleeping, bare-minimum housekeeping, helping the kids with homework—took up the rest. There was no time left for enjoying the people we loved, let alone having stimulating conversations.

Regardless of our original intentions, our priorities had become work and the absolute necessities required for getting everybody to work and school or day care. With companies placing greater demands on fewer employees to produce more, a work week of 50 or 60 hours is now the rule rather than the exception. Add to that a typical 30-minute commute, and most people are left with a couple of berserk hours each weekday to tend to family needs. We're willing to bet that this is *not* the life you envisioned for yourself back when you first set out to seek your fortune and start your family.

It certainly wasn't what we had pictured. When we compared the way we *wanted* to live our lives and take care of our families with how we were *actually* spending our time, the disparity was nauseating. We toyed with the idea of living in tents and eating beans and rice forever, if only we could be home most of the time. Fortunately, it hasn't come to that, but the point is that we were willing to make some sacrifices in exchange for time with our families.

There is no doubt about it. Making the move from two incomes to one is a big deal, and the decision shouldn't be taken lightly. Furthermore, *both partners must be committed to making it work*. It also helps if everyone in the family knows what changes to expect. Most two-income families who decide to have one partner quit a paying job have to cut back somewhere, but different families give up different things. Before making any sudden moves, you need to examine the pros and cons of living off one income. Again, these points will vary from family to family, but we've covered some of the biggies for you.

Some benefits of settling for half

Let's put aside the issue of money for a minute, and suppose you were to quit your job and become a full-time parent at home. Other than not having to go to a job away from home every day, what are some of the real benefits you can expect?

Reduced stress

If you're working full-time, like we were, you can realistically expect to lower the collective stress for the entire family once you decide to leave your job. You've heard the old adage: "If mother's happy, then everybody's happy." Well, the reverse is true, too: If mother's a complete basket case, then no one's life is worth living. Packing 36 hours of obligations into a 24-hour day is not just stressful for the mother who works (*and* may come home to shoulder 85 percent of the child rearing and the housekeeping responsibilities), it's hard on everybody in the house.

It's hard on the kids who are typically "on" for 10 or 11 hours each weekday while they are in school and/or day care, and who come home only to be fed, bathed, rushed through homework, and put to bed. It's hard on the man who sees his tired, cranky soul mate alone for approximately 35 seconds every evening before she falls into bed herself. Of course, all this applies to dads who go to work and share in the care of the kids and housekeeping, as well.

Families don't seem to have time to just *be* with each other anymore. Instead, families are instructed to spend "quality time" together. As best we can tell, "quality time" is something that you are supposed to schedule so that the people in your family actually pay some attention to each other for some portion of the week. If we are too busy and stressed out to have this happen naturally, then we are too busy. Being scheduled within an inch of our lives is harrowing, and in today's world the pressure never stops. Furthermore, stress tends to be contagious and can become so chronic that a two-day weekend isn't long enough to ease it. Even having one parent cut work back to part-time can free up enough time and energy to get the entire family back on a calmer track.

Better family relations and personal development

Another benefit you can expect—and we guarantee that it will happen—is that you will get to know your family, and yourself, better. As a result, your family will probably become closer. We have been a little amazed at this phenomenon because, like all parents with partners, we thought that we already had "close" families and that we knew everything there was to know about the people in them. For the most part, we did know our families *very* well. We just know them *better* now. Once a family has more unstructured time together, everyone has a greater chance to relax and simply become individuals—especially, it seems, the kids. We think this happens because once the family schedule is less rigid, everyone—even the parent who is still employed—has more free time to discover and pursue his or her own interests.

The freedom to choose

Along with a more flexible schedule comes greater freedom of choice. You and your family will decide how time is spent and which activities are priorities. If you decide that you want to drastically simplify your family's lifestyle, you can do it. If your family's passion is homemade bread, you can set aside time to make bread a couple of times each week. If your goal is simply to have a traditional family dinner every night, you can arrange your days to make that possible. Maybe you would like the time to read to your kids (or yourself) for an hour each day. Imagine not having to sacrifice a reasonable bedtime to do it! You can arrange to help out at the kids' school, volunteer in your community, or whatever else you've always wanted to do to make your piece of the world a better place. You will be in charge of your time and your family's time, rather than a slave to your day planner.

Along with the freedom of choice comes the freedom to manage your household in the best interest of your family. You'll have the time to work toward your family's goals whether that means having a year-round vegetable garden or managing your own retirement fund. You can participate in your children's education, or maintain your grocery budget. Instead of a place to sleep, eat, and do your laundry, your house will become family headquarters. Rather than pouring most of your energies into someone else's company and hoping you have some time left over each day for your family, you can apply your talents where you will have the greatest impact—at home.

No more day care

Finally, if you have children, the benefits of having one parent at home cannot be overstated. It is not our intent to offer a treatise on the evils of putting kids in day care, but we offer the following points for consideration. While many children seem to do fine in day care, how could they not be better off under the care of their own parents who love them and want what's best for them? Yes, there are some excellent day-care centers and many competent, loving childcare providers. But these people—with the possible exception of grandparents or other family members—are in the childcare business. Frankly, the only thing we imagine is less desirable than having a business raise our children would be having the government do it.

Pros and cons up close

If you've been a frenzied wreck for months on end, it can be difficult to really sort out your priorities. In fact, it can be difficult to think clearly at all anymore! Before you make the leap and quit your job, this exercise will help you assess the impact of the anticipated lifestyle changes ahead of you and help you decide where to focus your efforts first.

1. Together with your spouse, make detailed lists of all the legitimate pros and cons you can think of. You can use our benefits and stark realities as a guide, but the list will ultimately be your own. Be specific.
2. Rate each item from one to five, with five being "extremely important" and one being "not a big deal." Consider each item carefully, weighing it against the other items on the list.
3. Look at your completed, rated list. Find the items that you rated highest for each column, pro and con. On the pro side, the entries with the highest score are the priorities that deserve most of your time and energy. On the con side, the high scores will show you which drawbacks you will need to be most diligent about minimizing.
4. Keep your list and pull it out from time to time to compare your efforts with your original goals and priorities. You may need to revise the list every six months or so as circumstances change.

Some of the stark realities

There's good news and bad news: The bad news is that we are not magicians, and your reading this book will not automatically make switching to one income a completely painless process. The good news is that we are not magicians, and if we can make it work, so can you. As with the benefits, some of the stark realities of sending one parent home full-time will be specific to your family. But if you are anywhere near average, much of the following will apply to you:

♦ Without that second paycheck, some of the things that you thought were necessities (or even God-given rights) will become luxuries to be indulged in only occasionally. Sacrifices will have to be made. These may include: professional manicures, $50 haircuts, McDonald's Happy Meals, really good wine and imported beer, shopping sprees for designer clothing, fabulous vacations, or that new car every two years. You'll be watching your pennies, and that's that.

♦ Your kids will most likely have to make some adjustments, too! According to a survey of 2,400 children between the ages of 7 and 12 in six of the world's wealthiest countries, American kids are the "busiest shoppers." Of the American children surveyed, 55 percent reported that shopping was their favorite activity. ("Are All Children the Same?" by Nancy Ten Kate, *American Demographics*, June 1997.)

♦ No one tells a parent at home what to do or when to do it. This is a benefit for some people and a difficult adjustment for others. Either way, expect to have to fine-tune your self-discipline.

♦ Even if you're currently a working parent who comes home to do most of the housework, you will no doubt have even more housework to do. Having someone at home all the time tends to make the house messier than if everyone is gone all day. If you despise housework now, you probably won't suddenly develop a love of vacuuming or scrubbing the toilet once you quit your job, and you may find yourself doing it more often.

♦ The partner who continues to work will feel the additional pressure of being the sole breadwinner. The parent at home needs to remain sensitive to this. Diligent cost-cutting and having a contingency plan can lessen this phenomenon. (More on developing that plan in Chapter 5.)

- Spouses who quit work with the plan of returning to work someday may limit their career prospects to some extent. To minimize the damage, you may need to retain memberships in professional societies, and/or continue to network to stay abreast of trends in your field. If you're in an industry that requires continuing education to maintain certification, you will have to keep this up at your own expense.

- After the novelty wears off, the day-to-day life of a stay-at-home parent can be lonely and thankless at times. Unless some of your friends are stay-at-home parents already, sometimes you'll find yourself needing someone else to talk to. Expect to have to actively seek out and cultivate some new buddies.

The remainder of this book is dedicated to helping you cope with and overcome the negative side of having one partner stay home. We can't show you how to give up one paycheck without making some sacrifices, but we can help you make the sacrifices less noticeable. The payoff in the form of a sane and enjoyable home life is well worth it.

And finally...

We want to say it again: Unless you have no use whatsoever for that second paycheck, doing without it means you will be making some financial changes. Clarify your priorities, together, before making the decision. The key to converting to life on one income is *commitment* to a happier, healthier, saner lifestyle. And remember, this means *both* of you need to make the decision and the commitment— even the one who is still working.

Okay. Now you're ready to turn to Chapter 2 and take a look at how the second income is actually being spent.

What's *Really* Left of That Second Income?

When we left the work force, neither of us knew exactly how we would make ends meet. We knew that we would be getting rid of some expenses—such as childcare and extra gas. We also knew that while we were making salaries that covered those things and then some, it wasn't as if we had piles of money left over after paying monthly bills. Still, when we quit work, we didn't have anywhere near the shortfall we were expecting. After just a couple months of developing and refining new spending habits, we were amazed to find ourselves in pretty much the same financial position we had been with two salaries. We were also enjoying about the same standard of living, if not a better one. How could this be?

A big part of the answer lies in an honest appraisal of the second income itself, specifically, how much money it costs to have both of you working, especially if you have young children. We assumed that if we were being paid $25,000 a year, then we were bringing home more than $1,500 every month after taxes and other payroll deductions. We knew that it was costing us something to work, but we never bothered to look at work-related expenses beyond the huge expense of childcare. Once we were home and could see how much money our jobs had been costing us, we were floored.

In this chapter, we will be taking a closer look at costs directly associated with a second income. The object is to get an idea of how much your second income is worth after deducting expenses. After all, it doesn't matter how much you make, only how much makes it home.

We've used Mary's work-related spending for a typical year as an example. Of course, use these costs only as a guide. Your expenses may be higher or lower, depending on your situation. Mary has subtracted all of her expenses from $1,842, her monthly net earnings. You can see the actual figures in the chart on page 29, and the spending is detailed as follows. As you read, think hard about the money you spend because you work. Jot down your own expenses and subtract them from the monthly net of that second salary. Whatever is left is the amount of money the second income is actually contributing to the household. Warning: The answer may shock you.

The obvious costs

Childcare. Day care has become an expensive fact of life for the working parents of young children. If you pay for day care, it's probably your largest expense to come directly out of the second income. When Mary was working, she had one toddler, and one child in elementary school. Between full day care and after-school care, Mary was spending $125 each week during the school year. Her costs went up in the summer when her oldest child was in day care full-time.

Transportation. In order to bring home that second paycheck, you've got to show up for work. The cost of transportation varies widely depending on a number of factors. You may be lucky enough to have access to public transportation or a carpool, either of which can lessen your expenses considerably. Mary lives in a bedroom community, 40 miles from the city where she worked. Her parking was free and she paid no tolls, but she was spending at least $25 every week on gas. Her 80-mile round trip was putting an additional 20,000 miles on her car every year. This doesn't include the mileage to and from both day-care centers, or the extra trips she made running errands at separate times because her schedule was too hectic for her to do them all at once. In the end, Mary was racking up nearly 35,000 miles each year. That's a lot of oil changes (six per year, to be exact), to say nothing of additional tune-ups or how often she had to replace her tires. With the additional wear and tear, Mary needed a new vehicle every three or four years.

Clothing. Most offices have dress codes and most of us, both men and women, want to look reasonably fashionable. In some fields, image is extremely important and outfitting yourself for work can be expensive.

Mary's job required her to meet face-to-face with high-level executives. She would no more show up in a three-year-old suit for a first meeting with a CEO than she would go to church in a bikini. And then there were the accessories—purses, shoes, belts, and jewelry. Pantyhose alone can easily run (no pun intended) $20 each month, and that's buying the cheap ones at the grocery store! Mary typically spent at least $45 a month for her personal dry cleaning and about $30 a month on pantyhose. During the month we're using as an example, Mary found two suits on sale for $75 each. Luckily, she already owned blouses and shoes that she could wear with the new suits. While she didn't spring for a new suit every time she got paid, she did buy clothes for work on a regular basis, and it wasn't unusual for her to spend $50 to $100 over the course of the month.

The not-so-obvious costs

You know that you spend money on childcare, transportation, and work clothes, and you probably have a pretty good idea of how much these things are costing you. You have to spend money to make money, right? When people calculate the cost of the second income, they usually deduct these expenses and stop. Any other work-related expenses seem too small to make much of a difference. As it turns out, the "minor" expenses and the hidden costs were literally eating up more of Mary's paycheck than she ever thought possible.

Office food. Mary made an effort to take her lunch to work at least half the time. She went out to lunch once or twice a week with her office buddies, and would occasionally chip in a couple of dollars to have pizza delivered. She rarely spent more than $8 to lunch out. The only daily splurge Mary allowed herself was for breakfast. She never had time to eat before leaving home, and she figured that since she worked so hard, she deserved a perk here and there. Every day after dropping the kids off, she picked up a bagel or a pastry and a large, flavored coffee. Breakfast, plus a newspaper, came to about $4 a day. She also got a diet soda from the vending machine in her building nearly every day, but she just fished out 60 cents from the bottom of her purse for that. When she went back and tallied all her food expenses for the month, Mary was stunned to see that it added up to $162. (Ouch!)

Office socializing. Part of working is socializing with your co-workers and that's a good thing. A happy, friendly environment is conducive to productivity, and fitting into office culture is essential to professional well-being. Social expectations vary from company to company, but we have both worked in offices where being sociable required more than friendly chats over coffee and occasional drinks after work. We've seen all of the following occasions marked in the office with a gift or food offering, or both: graduation, retirement, getting a promotion, changing companies, being transferred, getting engaged, losing weight, having an illness, recovering from an illness, getting a divorce, and landing a big account. Birthdays and all the major holidays are also celebrated, of course. Weddings and births require full-fledged showers hosted by co-workers, often at the office during lunch. People at our jobs were getting married or having babies with astonishing frequency! Forgetting Boss' Day or Secretary's Day was reason enough to turn in your notice (especially Secretary's Day). This month Mary helped host a baby shower for one of the women in her office. Between helping with food, decorations, and buying a small gift, she spent $25.

Licenses, professional associations, and clubs. Many occupations require a license or certification to practice, which may need to be renewed every year or two. Fees vary. You can find a professional association for almost any profession, and in some fields membership is expected. Again, fees and expenses vary. Some people join local organizations like the Jaycees or the Kiwanis Club as a way to network with other members of the business community. Mary belonged to a sales club. There were no annual dues. Instead, the club met twice a month at a local restaurant, and she had to pay to attend the meeting. For $7.50, Mary could get a so-so brunch, listen to a ho-hum speaker, and exchange business cards with dozens of prospective clients. She rarely missed a meeting.

Groceries. When you work 30 or 40 hours a week you don't have much time left to devote to household concerns, and convenience starts to look like a necessity. You could hire someone to do all the cooking, cleaning, laundry, and yard work—which would be extremely convenient. Most people aren't willing or able to take on the expense. One place where working families are willing to pay for convenience is the grocery store. Mary was no exception. She certainly didn't have time in the evening to spend an hour or more cooking. If she couldn't get something from the refrigerator to the table in 30 minutes, she didn't buy it. As a result, she was relying heavily on frozen entrees, prepared foods from the supermarket deli, and packaged mixes. She knew that she could probably spend a little less at the grocery store if she did more cooking from scratch, but she simply did not have the time.

When Mary quit working, she stopped buying all the precooked and prepackaged food and shopped for ingredients instead. Her grocery bill dropped by $30 to $40 a week, even though her family was eating similar foods.

When Mary worked, sometimes even convenience food was too much trouble. About once a week, Mary was either so exhausted or so late leaving the office that she would grab a take-out dinner on the way home. Her husband usually picked up something for dinner once during the weekend to give Mary a break. For these meals they always got something fairly inexpensive like pizza, fried chicken, or fast food. This only cost about $15 per meal for a family of four. The couple didn't consider these pick-up meals as "eating out." They were just meals at home that Mary didn't have to prepare.

The costs you've never even considered

You probably have some costs that you may not even think twice about, like the ones outlined here.

Shopping as a lunchtime sport. Shopping was one of Mary's weaknesses and this month's spree wasn't unusual. Before lunch, Mary's shopping partner reminded her that a local department store was having a one-day sale. Mary needed a new suit for work and ladies' suits were half-price. She bought two. Because her friend was still shopping, Mary wandered into the men's department, where 100-percent silk ties were also half-price. After she bought a tie for her husband, Mary saw a table in the center aisle with girl's shoes on sale. She found a pair of famous-brand tennis shoes in her daughter Charity's size and bought them.

Her buddy was finished, but Mary couldn't possibly go home with something new for everyone except her youngest child! They took a detour into the children's department and found Paige a lightweight jacket marked down 25 percent. Mary had spent a total of $225. Remember, the only thing she really needed was a suit for work. The tie, shoes, and jacket weren't things that Mary's family needed, but rather deals she thought were too good to pass up. Had she been shopping by herself, Mary would have bought the suit and left. For some reason, Mary is always more conservative when she shops alone.

Pronto purchases. These are the things you end up paying too much for because you don't have time to do it any other way. You know the ones—last-minute presents for birthday parties; horribly expensive bakery cupcakes, rather than homemade ones for the school function; and those expensive in-town auto repairs opted for in a frenzy because the mechanic could have it done before lunch. For Mary, these kinds of things seemed to come up constantly. It's difficult to even determine how much these purchases cost her when she worked, but she estimates that she now spends at least 20-percent less on things like birthday presents simply because she never waits until the last minute anymore.

School lunches. When Mary worked, her school-aged daughter always bought school lunch. Lunch at Charity's school cost $2.25 per day. Mary didn't think twice about handing over $11.25 every week. This seemed like a small price to pay for one less thing to do.

Guilt purchases. These are the things you buy your children because you feel guilty. You may not do this, but many people fall into this habit without realizing it. Because Mary worked so far from home and had a job that required daily travel throughout a metro area, she was frequently an hour or more from her daughter's school. When school programs were held during the school day, which wasn't unusual, Mary was rarely able to attend. This month there was a lunchtime ceremony for children who met certain reading goals, and Charity was to receive an award. Knowing her daughter was disappointed that she could not make it, Mary stopped after work and bought her a gift. She also picked up something small for her youngest daughter so she wouldn't feel left out. This cost about $25.

A few *really* hidden costs of working

1. Business trips. How come an all-expense-paid business trip *always* ends up costing you so much of your own money? We estimate that we usually spent at least $150 for every week we spent out of town on business—some of which went for horribly overpriced airport gifts for the kids.

2. Fund raisers. It's hard to say no, particularly at the office. Even in companies with a "No Solicitation" policy, it's not unusual for parents to bring in the school's latest fund-raising effort. We've seen everything from raffle tickets to pizza kits. Girl Scout cookies were known to cause office stampedes.

3. Interoffice gambling. Who hasn't tossed a couple of bucks into the football pool, the baby-weight pool, or the Academy Awards pool?

4. Multilevel marketing products. There's one in every office. They're either selling cosmetics, home accessories, cleaning products, jewelry, plastic food containers, or toys.

5. Sunshine funds. Many companies request that employees kick in $1 per paycheck to be used for office parties, employee picnics, and the like.

The analysis

Of course, these aren't all of Mary's expenses, just the ones driven—either directly or indirectly—by the fact that she and her husband both worked. All of the expenses were within the normal range for Mary and her family, even the extra $75 dollars she spent during her lunchtime shopping spree (although usually she spreads this amount over more than one trip). Look at the following chart. Even though Mary makes $28,000, she is contributing less than $450 to her household each month. No wonder it wasn't as difficult as Mary thought to make ends meet once she quit her job! It doesn't seem quite worth it, does it? If you consider that Mary works 50 hours a week (not including her commute or any paperwork that she brings home), she only cleared $2.17 per hour this month. What's more, Mary's story isn't that unique. Your own numbers may not be any better.

Monthly Expenses for Second Income

Obvious costs

Full day care	340.00
After-school care	160.00
Gas	100.00
Oil change	20.00
Clothing (2 Suits, half price)	150.00
Dry cleaning for Mary	45.00
Pantyhose	30.00
Total obvious costs	**845.00**

Hidden costs

Lunches out	70.00
Breakfast and newspapers	80.00
Drinks from vending machine	12.00
Office socializing	25.00
Sales club	15.00
Sport shopping (not including suits)	75.00
Convenience groceries	120.00
Pick-up meals	96.00
School lunch	45.00
Guilt presents	25.00
Total hidden costs	**$563.00**
Total net monthly income (second salary minus payroll deductions)	**$1,842.00**
Total expenses	**$1,408.00**
Total amount second income contributes to bottom line	**$434.00**

One last thing to think about

We have discussed finances on the basis of net monthly income because that's how most people operate. In addition to taxes and social security, you may have medical insurance, 401(k) contributions, even charitable donations, that are be deducted from your paycheck.

You *Can* Afford to Stay Home With Your Kids

Of course, all this varies widely from individual to individual. Regardless of what is deducted from our salaries, we all have to make do on what's left. Still, a discussion of the second income and all its associated expenses wouldn't be complete if it didn't include a least a few words about federal income tax.

Back in the 1970s and early 1980s, it was fairly common for the entire second income and a healthy chunk of the first income to be consumed by federal income taxes. After the Reagan-era tax cuts, individual tax rates up to 50 percent gave way to rates of 15 percent and 28 percent. (Congress has since added higher rates for upper-income earners.) Now, 15 percent doesn't sound too bad, but what if you're a married couple filing jointly and the second income is pushing you into the 28 percent bracket?

Briefly, here's how it works. The federal government allows you to subtract certain deductions from your salary yielding a dollar amount called "taxable income." Your tax bracket is determined by your taxable income. Let's say that you're a family of four—two parents and two children—and Dad makes $50,000 a year. Using figures from 1998 and assuming the standard deduction and four personal exemptions, his taxable income is $29,400. This amount falls within the 15-percent tax bracket and the tax owed is $4,414.

Now, assume that Mom also works and she makes $30,000. Because all the allowable deductions have already been taken out of Dad's income, Mom's entire salary is subject to federal income tax. The second income carries no additional deductions or exemptions, only additional tax liability. When we add Mom's $30,000 to Dad's $29,400, we get $59,400 in taxable income and the tax owed jumps to $11,134. Even though Mom makes $20,000 *less* than Dad, her salary causes them to pay 150 percent *more* in federal income taxes than if they were taxed on his salary alone.

Here's why: Again, using the 1998 tax table for a married couple filing jointly, all taxable income up to $42,350 was taxed at a rate of 15 percent. Everything over $42,350 (in this case $17,050) was taxed at 28 percent, nearly double the tax rate. As if this weren't bad enough, because Mom's $30,000 salary would be taxable at 15 percent alone, her paycheck deductions are based on the 15-percent rate. This leaves an additional $2,216 (the extra 13 percent on $17,050) to be paid either via a reduced federal income tax refund or a check written to the IRS. Spread out over 12 months, this is *another* $184.67 each month that comes straight off the top of the second net income. In other words, even after subtracting all of your work-related expenses from your second salary's monthly paycheck, you may still have less realized income than you think. You'll have to look at the tax tables to find out.

The last year that Mary worked was 1996. That year her family had almost exactly the tax situation described here. If you drop her monthly contribution by another $180 each month, she is only bringing about $250 in realized income into the household monthly. She may have worked hard to earn a salary, $28,000, but she actually contributed about $3,000 a year to her household.

Chapter 3

Where Is Your Money Going?

By now, you're probably disappointed by how little that second income is netting you, especially considering the hoops you've been jumping through to get it. Once the second job goes, though, that paltry sum is going with it. The only reasonable thing to do is to make sure you can get along without the extra money. In this chapter, you are going to compare the primary income to your monthly expenses, and decide how to cover the shortfall.

The groundwork

For this project, you will need two small notebooks, one for each spouse. We suggest those tiny spiral-bound pads because they are small enough to fit in your pocket or purse. For one month, each of you will be keeping track of all the money you spend, and what you spend it on. This includes checks written for bills, the money handed to kids for lunch, the quarters you put in the newspaper machine, and absolutely everything else—even if you put it on a credit card. Don't round amounts off to the nearest dollar. Record the exact amount.

And as you note how the money was spent, be specific. You may not call any expenditure "miscellaneous" during this 30-day period. Keep receipts whenever possible, because some total purchases will need to be broken into different categories at the end of the month.

For example, if you spend $20 at the gas station or convenience store, you might have come away with $15 worth of gas, a soda, a bag of chips, and two lottery tickets. Gasoline and lottery tickets will ultimately land in separate categories. Yes, this is a pain in the neck and, no, you can't just estimate. Do it for one month. No cheating.

One month later...

So, how did your month go? Did you fill up your notebooks? Did you find yourself passing up some small purchases just so you wouldn't have to write them down? Did you start to feel self-conscious about how often you were reaching for your wallet?

Today you are going to categorize and total your spending for the past month. We did this for our sample family in the chart on pages 34 and 35. This is a month in the life of a real family, a few months before the mom quit her job. We'll call this family the Joneses. Below are the categories that we used and explanations of what each category includes. Stick with them as best you can, but if you need a few extra categories, add them. (Note: For simplicity, we have used round amounts in the example.)

Housing. Include your mortgage or rent, your homeowner's and mortgage insurance, as well as property taxes (pro rata). The Joneses live in a warm, humid, climate and contract with a pest control company for monthly extermination. If you have this or a similar expense related directly to your dwelling, include it here.

Utilities. The phone, electric, gas, water, and sewage bills, and garbage service (if you're billed for it) are all listed here. If you heat with wood or have oil delivered, don't forget to add that, too. Notice that the cable television bill is not in this category.

Groceries. Each and every trip to the grocery store is accounted for here. The big weekly trips are listed, as are the side trips for bread, milk, and anything you forgot. Use subheadings for each week. Also under a separate subheading, account for any meals you purchased instead of cooking dinner. This doesn't mean planned dinners out (which would be included in the "Entertainment" category). It means the meals you picked up for the sake of convenience, such as pizza, fast food, or a bucket of chicken.

Sample family monthly expenses

Before

Housing

Mortgage and insurance	935.00
Pest control	27.00
Total	**$962.00**

Utilities

Phone bill	92.00
Electric bill	85.00
Gas bill	64.00
Garbage service	15.00
Water bill	18.00
Total	**$274.00**

Groceries

Week #1	110.00
Week #2	149.00
Week #3	110.00
Week #4	107.00
Dinner pick-ups (eight)	96.00
Total	**$572.00**

Entertainment

Dinners/lunches out	150.00
Video rentals	42.00
Movies (for four)	30.00
Newspapers, magazines, and books	25.00
Cable television bill	32.00
Total	**$279.00**

Automobile Expenses

Car note #1	317.00
Car note #2	350.00
Gasoline and maintenance	200.00
Car insurance	124.00
Total	**$991.00**

Childcare

After-school care	160.00
Day care	340.00
Total	**$500.00**

School costs	
School lunches	45.00
One field trip	10.00
Total	**$55.00**
Allowances	
Older child	20.00
Younger child	4.00
Total	**$24.00**
Work-related expenses: Hers	
Lunches out	80.00
Coffee and pastry daily	40.00
Co-worker gifts	10.00
Total	**$130.00**
Work-related expenses: His	
Lunches out	80.00
Sales club dues	10.00
Total	**$90.00**
Charge cards	
MasterCard	100.00
Visa	45.00
Department store card	25.00
Total	**$170.00**
Clothing, sundries, and personal care	
Children's summer clothes	125.00
Dry cleaning	70.00
Total	**$195.00**
Medical costs	**$ 0.00**
Savings or investment accounts	
College fund #1	122.00
College fund #2	115.00
Total	**$237.00**
Total monthly expenses	**$4,474.00**
Monthly net income	
Salary #1	3,000.00
Salary #2	1,656.00
Total salary	**$4,656.00**
Surplus this month	**$182.00**

Entertainment. Any money you spend to entertain yourself or your family is listed here: cable television, movie rentals, movies at the theater (including concessions), dinners or lunches out, the Ice Capades, the indoor playground, lottery tickets (No, lottery tickets are *not* speculative investments!), and anything else spent in the name of entertainment. Include the cost of a baby-sitter as needed.

Automobiles/transportation. Car payments, car insurance, and gas all belong here. So do maintenance costs, parking or garage fees, and the monthly cost of public transportation, if any.

Childcare. List day-care fees, the cost of after-school care, or the money you pay to whomever takes care of your children while you are at work. If you purchase anything that you would not normally buy just to satisfy day-care requirements, list those expenses here, too. Examples include: disposable diapers you buy for day care, even if you use cloth at home, or those small jars of baby food you must send after your baby switches to table food at home.

School costs. Private or parochial school tuition belongs here. If your children buy lunch, breakfast, or snacks at school, list the monthly expense in this category. Also list incidental expenses such as field trips, school supplies, or school pictures.

Allowances. Enter the monthly amount of allowance you give your children.

Work-related expenses. This category will include the money each of you spends on lunch, including coffee and snacks if they are regular workday purchases. Also add the dues to any professional organizations, and all those contributions to various office gift funds. List each partner's expenses separately.

Charge cards. List each card and the amount you pay on it.

Clothing, sundries, and personal care. Even if you didn't buy any clothing this month, try to estimate what you might normally spend. Dry cleaning expenses go here. The money you spend on household items, such as detergent and paper goods, or personal items, such as shampoo and shaving supplies, can go in the grocery category if you purchase them there. Put them in this category if you purchase them separately. Haircuts and manicures also belong in this category.

Medical costs. If you pay for health insurance directly rather than via a payroll deduction, list it here. Otherwise, do not include any amount deducted from your paycheck for health insurance, but do include any out-of-pocket medical expenses such as your copayment at the doctor's office, and any prescription medications or medical supplies.

Savings and investments. Again, for our purposes here, we will not include any money that is direct-deposited or drafted straight out of your paycheck into a savings account, 401(k) plan, or anything similar. You are only looking at payments made out of cash flow. For example, include money you deposit into your savings account, an account at a brokerage firm, or a pre-paid tuition fund.

Life insurance. Note that the Joneses currently have no entry for life insurance. This is because both Mr. and Mrs. Jones have low-cost life insurance as an employee benefit, and the monthly premium is a payroll deduction. However, once Mrs. Jones stops working, they will need to get some inexpensive coverage on her. They plan to buy term life insurance, and will discuss the amount of coverage with their accountant. They will shop around for the best price. They estimate that they will spend a maximum of $40 a month on term life for Mrs. Jones.

Monthly net income. For our purposes, we are looking at net income rather than gross income. For now, forget what is deducted for taxes, insurance, 401(k) plans, or anything else that your employer deducts from your check.

What?! We spent $100 on pizza?!

Can you believe it? Were you surprised to see how the Joneses spent their money? Spending—or saving—for college funds is great, but the family also spent $96 on take-out and that was *on top of* nearly $500 in groceries *and* a few dinners at restaurants. Yikes! Did you notice their entertainment category? They spent $300, and didn't do *anything* especially entertaining.

What's that? You say that your family's monthly spending looks slightly screwy, too? Well, take heart. Actually the Joneses' spending this month doesn't look unusual. Although they spent quite a bit on food, they don't have to account for multiple trips to discount stores or needless shopping sprees at the mall. In fact, they thought they were spending carefully. Still, the Joneses were able to cut their monthly budget enough for Mom to quit work just a few months later. So, stop chewing your fingernails and go sharpen your pencil! When you come back, we'll see where you can tighten up your monthly expenses.

But first, a few things to think about

You probably already have an idea of where your budget is flabby. Everyone thinks about spending money wisely. Features on saving money appear endlessly in magazines and on the morning news programs, while books on better money management fly off bookstore shelves. So why do we still waste so much money?

We waste money for several reasons. Often we're simply not paying attention to what we spend or how quickly the small purchases add up. Think about all those cups of coffee we buy on the way to work. Who knew they were adding up to $20 or $30 dollars every month? Sometimes we buy something simply because it exists and we don't have one yet. How many times have you actually *used* your pasta maker? You've managed fine for all these years without an electronic personal organizer. Do you really need one now?

We willingly pay a premium for convenience because we're so pressed for time. What about those cute little boxes of fruit juice with the straws attached? Ounce for ounce, those little boxes cost nearly *five times* as much as the fruit juice concentrate found in the freezer section. Is it really that difficult and time-consuming to pour juice into a cup or thermos?

The entire advertising industry exists solely to point out (or dream up) reasons why we should not keep our money in our wallets. The most common reason we waste so much money—and the advertisers and manufacturers know it—is *habit*. Remember: The focus of streamlining your expenses is not about going without things your family needs. Instead, it's about shedding wasteful habits and cultivating new ones so you can have one parent at home full-time.

Here's another thing to remember as you're cutting your spending: Some cuts may be considered temporary. Most of us are carrying at least some consumer debt, which will eventually be paid off. As you eliminate debt, you free up some of your cash flow. Your rewards are greater financial security and greater flexibility within your budget.

Scaling down with the Joneses

Like your family, the Joneses needed to know how far they could stretch their primary income. After some creative thinking, they came up with the plan shown in the chart on page 40 and 41. As you look at the Joneses' monthly financial makeover, notice the impact that minor adjustments have on their bottom line. The only "large" expense that they've taken out of the budget is childcare.

Scrutinize your family's expenses to see where you can save money. Be creative. Be ruthless. Look at each expense as if it were the one thing standing between you and your goal. Remember that $100 is $100, whether it's all in one place or a couple of dollars in 50 places, and don't regard any expense as too small to matter. Here are the cuts the Joneses made, plus a few extra ideas to get you started:

Housing. Most families simply leave this category alone. However, if you own your home and interest rates drop more than 1.5 percent below your current mortgage rate, you may be able to save money despite the cost of refinancing. If you have other expenses connected directly to your dwelling, make sure you're getting the best deal for your money. The Joneses have a yearly contract with an exterminator, but when the contract expires they will handle the pest control themselves.

Utilities. After doing some research and reviewing their utility bills, the Joneses decided that they could reduce their total utility costs by about 20 percent. Gas and electric companies usually have pamphlets loaded with ideas for reducing usage, and may even conduct a household energy audit for a small fee. Call your utility companies and ask. You can also check Chapter 10 for ways to reduce your utility bills immediately. Because the Joneses have the option to forego trash pickup, they now take their garbage to the processing plant themselves.

Groceries. The Joneses decided to cut grocery costs by 25 percent and to stop getting take-out meals, except as an occasional treat. This leaves them with a grocery budget of about $90 per week. After examining last month's grocery receipts and taking a price-comparison

Sample family monthly expenses

After

Housing

Mortgage and insurance	No Change	$935.00
Pest control	No Change	27.00
Total		**$962.00**

Utilities

Phone bill	Less 23.00	69.00
Electric bill	Less 17.00	68.00
Gas bill	Less 9.00	55.00
Garbage service	Less 15.00	0.00
Water bill	Less 1.80	16.20
Total	**Less 65.80**	**$208.00**

Groceries

Week #1	Less 27.50	82.50
Week #2	Less 37.25	111.75
Week #3	Less 27.50	82.50
Week #4	Less 26.75	80.25
Dinner pick-ups (eight)	Less 96.00	0.00
Total	**Less 215.00**	**$357.00**

Entertainment

Dinners/lunches out	Less 110.00	40.00
Video rentals	Less 32.00	10.00
Movies (for four)	Less 30.00	0.00
Newspapers/magazines/books	Less 25.00	0.00
Cable television bill	No Change	32.00
Total	**Less 197.00**	**$82.00**

Automobile expenses

Car note #1	No Change	317.00
Car note #2	No Change	350.00
Gasoline and maintenance	Less 66.00	134.00
Car insurance	No Change	124.00
Total	**Less 66.00**	**$925.00**

Childcare

After-school care	Less 160.00	0.00
Day care	Less 340.00	0.00
Total	**Less 500.00**	**$0.00**

School costs		
School lunches	Less 36.00	9.00
One field trip	No Change	10.00
Total	**Less 36.00**	**$19.00**
Allowances		
Older child	No Change	20.00
Younger child	No Change	4.00
Total		**$24.00**
Work- related expenses: Hers		
Lunches out	Less 80.00	0.00
Coffee and pastry daily	Less 40.00	0.00
Co-worker gifts	Less 10.00	0.00
Total	**Less 130.00**	**$0.00**
Work-related expenses: His		
Lunches out	No Change	80.00
Sales club dues	No Change	10.00
Total		**$90.00**
Charge Cards		
MasterCard	Add 15.00	115.00
Visa	Add 6.75	51.75
Department store card	Add 3.75	28.75
Total	**Add 25.50**	**$195.50**
Clothing, sundries, and personal care		
Children's clothes	Less 50.00	75.00
Dry cleaning	Less 40.00	30.00
Total	**Less 90.00**	**$105.00**
Medical costs	**Add 15.00**	**$15.00**
Savings or Investment Accounts		
College fund #1	No Change	122.00
College fund #2	No Change	115.00
Savings account	Add 50.00	50.00
Total	**Add 50.00**	**$287.00**
Total spending cuts		**$1,209.30**
Total spending after cuts		**$3,264.70**
Net salary #1		**$3,000.00**
Deficit this month		**$264.70**

trip through the supermarket, the Joneses realized they could easily live within this budget if they made the following changes in their shopping and eating habits:

1. Stop buying prepackaged items and frozen dinners.
2. Stop buying expensive snack foods, and replace them with fruit, crackers, and cheese.
3. Buy and consume only half as much soda, beer, and wine.
4. Buy store brands, rather than more expensive national brands, whenever possible.
5. Look at weekly sales fliers, and plan meals around good deals.
6. Take a list to the grocery store and stick to it.

As simple as this plan sounds, the Joneses have easily kept to their budget and are eating better than ever. They are also saving $200 per month.

If you ultimately find that you need to make deep spending cuts, this is a category to keep in mind. We know of families who spend substantially less on food than the Joneses. Whatever you decide to do about groceries, set a budget and stick with it.

Entertainment. The Joneses decided that they could do without spending so much money on entertainment every month. They budgeted $40 for eating out in restaurants. They can use it for a family dinner, an inexpensive lunch date for Mom and Dad (including a little baby-sitting), or whatever else they can think of. The Joneses budgeted $10 for video rentals—one pick per person per month—and now borrow movies from the public library for free. The Joneses use their library more often. In addition to movies, they check out books and read magazines at the library instead of buying them. Mr. Jones receives the newspaper at his office and brings it home rather than having another one delivered there. Instead of afternoons at a matinee or an indoor playground, they can always go to a public park or even their own backyard.

The only expense in this category that the Joneses didn't cut was the cable bill. But this doesn't mean you have to do the same. If your local channels are fuzzy without cable, you can buy an antenna at an electronics store that will greatly enhance your reception. This

antenna will pay for itself in a month or two at the most. Without cable, you may find that your family watches TV less, and this carries a
financial benefit as well: The less you are exposed to advertising, the
less likely you are to buy (or want) things you don't need.

Sit down as a family and discuss which activities bring the most
enjoyment. Brainstorm about inexpensive ways to do those things
that your family really loves. Decide how much money you can put
toward entertainment right now, and stick to it as long as necessary.

Automobiles/transportation. If you rely on public transportation, your transportation expenses already may be as low as possible.
Otherwise, you can almost certainly save some money in this category
once one of you quits work. Many of us consider car payments inevi-
table, just like death and taxes. As a result, most families have at
least one car note, if not two. The Joneses are no exception, but they
plan to keep the car payments as they are for now. Maybe you can
easily handle your payments on one salary. If so, great. If not, here
are some options:

Share a car. Some two-car families may be able to manage with
just one vehicle. If it's possible for either partner to take public transportation, having only one car can work out beautifully. Remember
that taking public transportation also saves money for parking. Is it
possible for the at-home spouse to drive the working spouse to and
from work? Maybe the at-home spouse can do without the car during
working hours. Only your family can decide whether one of these
alternatives—or a combination of them—will work for you.

Buy down. If you're still making payments but have a fair
amount of equity in your car, you may be able to sell it and buy a good
used car with the proceeds. Resist any temptation you might have to
lease a new car. While you might be able to lower your monthly payments, when the lease is up you will have no trade-in and no car. This
tends to leave people in a lurch, which is possibly what the car company intended. Once you're in this predicament, the car dealer can
rescue you by either letting you buy the car you've already paid scads
of money for, or leasing you a brand-new one.

Gas and maintenance. Once one of you quits driving to and
from work every day, your gas and maintenance cost will likely go
down automatically. Make sure it stays down by planning to run

several errands per trip rather than one at a time, and by keeping your eyes open for the best gas prices in your area. Look into carpooling with other families in your neighborhood for school, extracurricular activities, or work. Keep your tires properly inflated. Don't shirk regular maintenance. If either one of you is mechanically inclined, pick up a good, comprehensive automobile maintenance manual. It will pay for itself after a few backyard oil changes.

Car insurance. Driving fewer miles each day may lower your insurance rates. Be sure to notify your insurance company once one of you quits driving to work. This won't save a fortune, but it should knock off a few dollars per month. Make sure you're not overinsured. For example, if you have health insurance, you don't need personal injury coverage on your car insurance. Also, the lower your deductible, the higher your premiums; so you should carry the highest deductible you can manage. If you do decide to buy a less expensive car, your insurance may drop dramatically, and, of course, you don't have to insure any car that you get rid of and don't replace.

Childcare. POOF! It's gone.

School costs. Even public school is probably costing you more than you realized—and not just in taxes.

Tuition. If your children attend private or parochial school, you have tuition to pay. Consider alternatives. Could your child go to public school? Remember that once one of you is home, you can make time to personally supplement your child's education if you feel it's necessary. Many families are opting to school their children at home. Homeschooling isn't for everyone, but academically speaking, homeschooled children as a group test on par with or above their preparatory school counterparts. Homeschooling parents report spending much less time teaching each day than we would have thought—from about two to three hours for elementary-age children, declining to 15 minutes here and there for high schoolers. By the time homeschoolers reach high school, most receive more instruction from books and videos than from Mom or Dad.

If your child must stay in private school, don't hesitate to ask the school about scholarships. Many offer some form of scholarship, and parochial schools may offer financial aid, especially if religious practice requires that the child attend through a given age.

School food. In the Joneses' "before" budget, you may have noticed $45 for school lunches. Their school-aged daughter was buying lunch every day at $2.25 a pop. This is high even for school lunch, but that's the price at their school. They realized that they could save money if they packed their child's lunch, but *not* if they bought pre-packaged lunch items and juice boxes. Their daughter now takes a lunch consisting of home-prepared food, cookies and/or fruit. They have budgeted enough for milk money and the occasional purchase of a favorite cafeteria lunch.

Field trips, school pictures, and book clubs. Usually, field trips occur only once or twice a year, with nominal cost and plenty of notice. School pictures are an institution, but they can be expensive and they don't always turn out well. If you have current pictures you like of your child and the quality of the school photos isn't great, don't feel like you have to buy them. (Although this may sound like heresy, it's not illegal—we swear!) Book clubs may offer inexpensive books, but consider whether the cost is worth it. The selection is very limited, and books offered may be below your child's reading level. In this case, it might make more sense to check with your library or spend a little extra money buying the appropriate books.

Allowance. The Joneses believe in giving their children an allowance. Their 4th-grader gets $5 per week and their preschooler gets $1 per week. If you haven't been giving allowances, consider budgeting for it. See Chapter 9 for advice on allowances.

Work-related expenses. The Joneses' plan is to have Mrs. Jones quit work, so her expenses aren't an issue. Mr. Jones usually spends about $20 each week on lunch, and spends $10 monthly on dues for his sales club. For now, the Joneses intend to keep these expenses as they are. They know, however, that if money gets tight this is an easy place to save at least $80 each month by having Mr. Jones take a lunch to work.

If you're the partner who will continue to work, take a look at your own work-related spending. Are you spending money daily on coffee and snacks? Snacks are easy to bring from home. If coffee isn't available at your workplace, can you bring a thermos from home? If you buy a coffee maker for your office, it would pay for itself within a month. If you have access to a refrigerator, you can bring soft drinks and juices from home. Many workplaces now have microwaves available, which expands your options for lunch.

Charge cards. If you always carry a balance on your credit cards, you will save money by paying them off. This is a universal truth. Here's another one: If you never remit more than the minimum payment, you will be paying on your credit cards almost forever. The Joneses have actually increased their credit card payments by 15 percent. They know that this will help them pay off the cards sooner, and will save them money in interest in the long run. As one card is paid in full, the budgeted payment will be applied toward the remaining debt. They have no plans to continue using the cards on a regular basis. When these debts are finally gone, the Joneses will have an extra $195 each month.

Look at your family's credit card debt, if any. Are you using the cards regularly and carrying a balance most months? This is a sign that you've probably been living beyond your means. (If that last sentence makes you feel defensive and indignant, you've definitely been living beyond your means, and you're not alone.) Credit cards can be handy in an emergency, but they are a real problem for many families. If you can't resist the temptation to use your credit card, cut them up. If you must have a credit card, keep one major card and put it in a safe-yet-inconvenient place. Destroy the rest. And pay the darned things off.

Clothing, sundries, and personal care. These purchases vary tremendously from family to family, and probably month to month for each family.

Obviously, we all have to have clothes. What we do not have to have is brand-new, expensive designer clothes every few weeks. The first rule of spending less on clothing is to take care of what you already have. Don't wear your good clothes for dirty jobs. Regardless of what you see in catalogues and ads, it's obviously not a good idea to do the gardening in a $100 linen dress! Keep up with mending, treat stains promptly, and use the appropriate temperature and cycle settings when doing the laundry. Don't forget that your neighborhood shoe repair shop can work wonders on heels and soles, and even things like leather purses. When you do have to buy something, make sure you're getting your money's worth. Look for well-made, classic clothing in long-wearing fabrics. Shop around for good prices, but remember that "cheaper" and "less expensive" aren't necessarily synonymous. A pair of $25 jeans that can be worn for a year and then passed down to a younger sibling (even as cut-off shorts) are a better buy than $18 jeans that are falling apart in four or five months and have to be replaced.

Dry cleaning is another regular expense for many people. If the spouse who will be quitting wears business clothes to work, then your dry cleaning bills will probably go down automatically. The Joneses' bill will be cut by more than half. They can realize an even greater savings if Mr. Jones stops taking his dress shirts to the dry cleaners, if they hand-wash delicate washables at home, and if they wear washable clothing whenever possible.

The Joneses buy toothpaste, detergent, paper products, and the like at the grocery store, so those things appear in their grocery category. While detergent (or whatever) may be a few cents cheaper at the discount store, by the time they drive there and take advantage of the other great discounts they see, they've spent more money than if they had picked up the detergent with the groceries in the first place.

Regardless of where you make these purchases, make sure you're not throwing your money away. It is a scientific fact that $9 shampoo won't make you look like the model in the picture any faster than shampoo that costs $3. You don't need 25 different cleaning products to clean your home. A few basic ones will do. Buy generic brands whenever you can. Honestly, if bleach is bleach (and it is), why pay extra for the name on the outside of the bottle? And don't buy any of this sundry stuff if you already have something at home that will do the same job.

If you have to have a manicure, learn to do it at home. Learn to cut your kid's hair. There are several very good books and videotapes that teach haircutting step-by-step. If you refuse to give up expensive salon haircuts, consider getting trims at less expensive places and only splurge on major cuts and reshaping a couple of times each year.

Medical costs. The Joneses have their health insurance through Mr. Jones's employer, so the paycheck will not change. The Joneses are fortunate in that everyone in their family is healthy. Visits to the doctor's office are infrequent. Still, they have decided to budget $15 each month in case someone gets sick. The Joneses' health insurance is an HMO, and $15 will cover their co-payment for one office visit and one prescription each month. They know they probably won't need to use this money every month, so they will slowly build up a medical expense cushion. Consider your family's health and medical needs and create a plan that will enable you to seek medical treatment whenever necessary.

Savings or investment accounts. The Joneses have a college fund set up for each of their two children, but they were not putting anything into a savings account. They will continue the same payment into the college funds and will start putting $50 into savings every month. No, $50 isn't a fortune, but it's better than the $0 they were saving before. You need to save something from your income each month, and this should be the very first check you write when you get paid. The family will make their savings deposit on payday and they simply will not spend any more than what's left over. If your company offers direct deposit, arrange to have your savings contribution deposited straight into your savings account.

How much money should your family have in savings? Some experts say six months' salary, while others say a paycheck or two and a credit card for emergencies. The rest say something in between. The smartest thing to do is talk to an accountant. A good accountant will look at your situation, expenses, and goals, and help you determine the best answer for your family.

Net income

We've based all budgeting on net income figures because what you have to work with is the total you actually receive in your paycheck. However, you still need to look at what's being deducted from your salary. Avoid the temptation to over-withhold for income tax purposes. Getting a fat tax return each spring seems like a great windfall, but all you've done is let the government use your money that you never owed in the first place. An accountant will tell you that your best bet is to claim your deductions so you just meet your tax liability, or even owe the government a few dollars in April. Just make sure you pre-pay at least 90 percent of your federal income tax to avoid penalty.

Compare the take-home pay of the spouse who will continue working with your new budget. At this stage you will have one of two scenarios:

1. Your primary net income is greater than your proposed budget total, in which case you can skip the rest of this chapter and go straight to Chapter 4.

2. Your proposed budget total is greater than your primary net income, in which case you need to keep reading.

Closing the gap

Many families still have a monthly deficit after reworking the budget. This doesn't mean you both have to work forever, it means you need to invest more time and energy toward getting your expenses completely under control.

Look at how much of a gap you have. Did you leave anything in the budget on a "let's see" basis? If so, go back and take those expenses out. You can also take another look at the categories that have the most flexibility (such as entertainment or groceries), and trim them a little more. Once you've wrung the last errant nickel out of your budget, see if you still have a gap. If you do, it's time to take a closer look at debt.

Breaking the ties that bind

The overwhelming majority of families are carrying some form of debt. Some debts are perfectly understandable. Mortgages, medical debts, and student loans aren't frivolous expenses. But equally common are car notes, boat payments, spontaneous credit card purchases, no-interest-until-the-cows-come-home deals on living room furniture, or any of the other things you can "buy" without paying for it on the spot. If you can't make ends meet, it's probably debt that's tying your family to two incomes. Sure, you could afford the payments when you signed the papers, but now you're stuck letting a two-year-old car and an eight-piece dining room suite dictate how you live your life. This, of course, is ridiculous and needs to be fixed.

Take a look at all your monthly debt payments. Choose one or more that, once paid, will free up enough cash to cover your monthly deficit. These are the debts you're going to attack. Here are our three favorite methods for paying off debt. You can choose one or a combination, or devise your own plan. You can use all three plans in succession. Take some time, do some research, play with the numbers, and decide what's best for your family. Remember your goal is to reduce the demands on your monthly cash flow so you can meet your needs and obligations with only the primary net income. You want to get one parent in the home as quickly as possible.

The fire sale. If you've got some money you can spare from savings, put it toward a debt. Has your brother-in-law been lusting after your big-screen television? Sell it to him for the amount you owe on it and settle the account. Put your entire tax return or any bonuses toward paying off a debt. Hold a garage sale and put the entire proceeds toward what you owe. Put an ad in the paper for the boat, snowmobile, ski, or scuba equipment. Do any one of these things. Do all of these things. Do anything you can think of to come up with some cash as long as it's legal, moral, and doesn't involve going further into debt. Be creative and think, think, think. Depending on the amount of the debt you're getting rid of, this method can work alone or in conjunction with another tactic.

The squeeze play. Here's how it works: You both keep working, but immediately begin to live on your new single-income budget. Of course you'll still have any childcare expenses and probably the cost of transportation to the second job, but everything else goes. Start packing lunches and cut back on groceries, dry cleaning, entertainment, utilities—the works. It may be tough, but it's temporary. Use each and every dime you save to beef up the regular monthly debt payments. This is the way the Joneses did it. They decided to pay off Mrs. Jones's car, which was $350 per month. By biting the bullet and sticking to all the budget cuts except childcare and gas, they were able to put an additional $500 each month toward the loan. When they paid it off six months later, Mrs. Jones quit work and they had about $80 left over monthly. They also have more in savings than they did when both were working. That was a year and a half ago. Since then, the Joneses have paid off their credit cards, and now have more than $250 in discretionary income each month. This plan can be very effective as long as everyone pitches in and you can satisfy the debt within a short time—say six to eight months.

The partial retreat. In this case, the parent who ultimately will be at home stops working full-time and finds something part-time. The idea is to alleviate the need for childcare, begin to live on your new budget, and be able to put the entire second income toward clearing up an obligation or two.

Maybe your boss would let you cut back to part-time. Do you think your job can be accomplished with reduced hours in the office and part-time at home? If so, write up a proposal and present it to your supervisor. If the children are in school, find a job where you can work from 8 a.m. until noon or two o'clock. If the primary wage earner works regular business hours, then you can take a position working a couple of nights per week and the weekends.

Perhaps you can scare up enough freelance work (tutoring, book-keeping, sewing, landscaping, or whatever you can do with very little or no investment) to earn the equivalent of a part-time paycheck. Take a look at what part-time jobs are available and get a feel for the hourly wage you can expect to earn. Use this to determine how much net income you can generate. If you can earn enough to cover your shortfall with money left over to pour into bills, this will be an excellent short-term solution. If you will only be making enough money to make ends meet, you'll be on this plan until your budgeted payments resolve the debt. Some families find that this arrangement allows them to meet all of their goals and they settle into it permanently.

Drastic measures

In the 1950s, the average family of four lived in a house that was just under 1,000 square feet. Today a master bedroom suite may take up about half that. Throw in a family room, formal living room, eat-in kitchen, formal dining room, a bedroom for each child, an office, the guest room, extra bathrooms, walk-in closets, foyer, and a bonus room over the garage, and you're talking a big house with a big mortgage or lease. If your house is the obstacle between your family and the life your family wants, consider moving. Regardless of how much more time you may all have together or how much you've all relaxed your new daily schedule, you will not enjoy your life if you lie awake every night wondering how you'll pay the house note.

If you move to a smaller place, you'll probably save money on utilities and maintenance, as well as housing. Talk to your accountant about the tax implications of buying down, and keep in mind that property taxes and homeowner insurance are likely to cost less, too. You might even make a bundle unloading extra sofas, chairs, and bedroom furniture you no longer need!

The idea of selling the house you've worked so hard to buy may be shocking, but if you're faced with either letting the house go or letting your dream of a saner, family-oriented lifestyle remain merely a dream, the decision won't be that difficult. We promise that years from now, you won't find yourself on your deathbed moaning, "If only we'd had a mudroom."

What are you waiting for?

Some families will be able to get their finances in hand and their new lifestyle underway within a few months. Other families may be in transition for a year or so. Whatever your time line—but particularly if it's longer than a two week's notice—don't wait for a "better" time to begin. Projects that we postpone until all circumstances are perfect have an appalling tendency to never get started at all. The best time to do whatever it takes to make your family's life better is today. Get moving!

Part Two

What Will It Be Like When I Get There?

Chapter 4

What It Takes
to Make It
Work

Chapter 3 was long and it was all about money. When a family converts from two incomes to one, money is usually a big issue. But money is not the whole picture. In fact, as strange as it may sound, money isn't even the most important factor governing your success. This chapter explores the skills and attitude adjustments that, for us, have been crucial for beginning and maintaining an enjoyable single-income lifestyle. Please note that in researching this book, we spoke with a lot of people who have also made the change from two incomes, and *every one* of them described *at least* one of the following factors as instrumental to their success.

Commitment: Trying to do things right

Living on one income requires commitment. We hear the word commitment thrown around a lot, but do we really stop and think about what it means? If a friend invites us to lunch but we have already agreed to baby-sit the neighbor's kids, we say we can't go because we have a prior *commitment*. When politicians try to drum up support for a tax increase, they assure us that they're only asking because of a *commitment* to the excellence in public education, or some such thing. When two people marry, they make a *commitment* to each other. In essence, they promise to keep their vows and to stay married no matter what. Here's the way we see commitment:

The Snyder/Wyckoff Theorem of Commitment

A commitment is a promise you make—primarily to yourself, but possibly to others, as well—in order to achieve a goal even though, at times, you will probably want to forget the whole thing.

Commitment, therefore, is a double-edged sword. It's both a promise to advance toward a goal and a promise to overcome any obstacles that might keep you from reaching that goal.

The traditional marriage commitment makes a nifty illustration. Notice how the vows include the phrases, "for better or for worse," "in sickness and health," and "until death do you part." Gloomy as they sound, those phrases are in there for a reason. Long ago, someone realized that even though couples begin marriage with the best intentions, from time to time things will happen to make them want to throw in the towel and do something else entirely. That's just the way life is. Knowing that we're only human, our religious institutions remind everybody right in the middle of the wedding that every day wouldn't be blissful. The couple then promises to stick it out in spite of everything. The bride and groom are required to make promises *because* the road to happiness is likely to be riddled with potholes.

First Corollary to the Snyder/Wyckoff Theorem of Commitment

Commitment to a given goal is only necessary if your other aims and desires—no matter how compelling—have the potential to wreck the whole program.

When we each quit our jobs, we did it because we were desperate to spend more time with our families. We had done nothing to get ready financially, and we were home only on a trial basis. Life got better immediately. Time was no longer something we raced against, but a resource at our disposal. From the very first day at home our children behaved better, we got decent amounts of sleep, our husbands said we were nicer, and we felt like we had a handle on things for the first time in years. We were off the treadmill and we never wanted to get back on. When we became *committed* to making our new lifestyle last, preserving that lifestyle became a priority.

One thing became obvious. We could not continue to spend money at the rate we were used to spending it. For the first few months at home, we weighed every spending decision against our commitment. The commitment forced us to hunt through the pantry for low-fuss dinner ingredients when we would've preferred to call out for pizza. Our commitment kept us out of the mall, even in the face of acute shopping withdrawal. Thankfully, within a few months we didn't have to struggle to honor our commitment. It was a habit.

Second and Final Corollary to the Snyder/Wyckoff Theorem of Commitment

If you make a commitment to a given goal and certain actions pursuant to the attainment of that goal become a pain in the neck, the commitment itself may be the *only* thing that hauls you through the days when your neck is killing you.

If you're still reading this book, then you're most likely still planning to send one parent home full-time. You probably had to make some budget cuts when you worked your way through Chapter 3. The trick to making the single-income lifestyle financially feasible is to spend less than you earn. Actually, spending less than what you earn is the trick to solvency, regardless of your lifestyle or income. This requires commitment, especially if spending less than you earn means spending less than you're accustomed to. Even if you can stick to a budget with no problem, you may find that occasional feelings of isolation nag at you. In this case, a commitment to make time for outside activities will keep you from going batty. Maybe your obstacle is something we don't mention at all. Be honest about your weaknesses. In addition to your commitment to become a single-income family, make whatever additional commitments are necessary to comfortably maintain your family's new status.

A healthy dollop of anti-consumerism

A few years ago, Malia had an epiphany involving a coffeepot. She'd had the same boring, discount store, drip-style, coffee maker since college. When her coffee maker died after years of faithful service, Malia bought a fancy European coffee maker that she had seen in all the glossy magazines and all the best stores. It set her back nearly $100.

She was thrilled with her new coffee maker. She loved the way it looked so sleek sitting on her kitchen counter. She felt sophisticated just owning it—the coffee maker was tangible proof of her superb taste. For a solid week, she bounded out of bed to make coffee. She even bought an equally sleek, equally European, electric coffee grinder. "Nothing but the freshest ground, designer coffee for *my* coffee maker. Anything less, of course, would be ridiculous."

Within a few weeks, Malia was occasionally grabbing regular coffee when she bought groceries. Trips to the coffee shop for gourmet beans was inconvenient, and gourmet coffee costs three times more than supermarket coffee. After a couple of months, she stuck the grinder in a closet, because she wasn't using it and she kept knocking the darn thing over in her tiny kitchen. Sometimes she had to do without her morning coffee altogether, because her regular grocery store didn't carry the special, cone-shaped filters (30 for $3), and she often forgot to make a special trip to the upscale grocery. Finally, when it was about a year old, the wonderful coffee maker died. Malia drove straight to the discount store and—for $35—bought a regular, name brand, coffee maker (with automatic timer and drip-stop feature) and a two-year supply of filters. Malia had learned several things:

♦ Price isn't necessarily an indicator of quality.

♦ Expense and availability of necessary accessories must be taken into account.

♦ You are not what you wear, drive, live in, or make coffee with, despite what you've heard.

♦ Although buying the trappings of wealth and sophistication won't make you wealthy or sophisticated, it may help you go broke.

You probably have something in a closet like Malia's coffee maker. Between inflated expectations, relentless advertising, and an ever-increasing array of consumer goods, it's no wonder that consumerism has gotten completely out of hand. Having grown up during times of relative prosperity, many 25- to 45-year-olds have never known what it's like *not* to be able to go out and buy most of the things they want. We don't remember (or realize) that when our parents were young adults and starting out, they budgeted for necessities and saved for luxuries.

Television has further warped our expectations. The average 35-year-old has spent a staggering number of hours in front of the television. In TV land, the hip and wealthy reign. It seems everyone lives in nifty apartments with cool stuff. Their hair is expensively coifed and clothes are always the very latest fashion. People on television have it all, and many of us actually spend more time visiting TV land than we spend seeing how other real people live. How many of us unconsciously base our material expectations on the advertiser-driven fantasy world of television?

This is the Information Age. Television, radio, newspapers, and magazines have always been prevalent in our lives. Although these are the chief vehicles of advertising, they aren't the only ones. There are billboards. There are high-profile, corporate-sponsored events. There are high-profile professional athletes who have become human billboards. It's no secret that companies pay dearly for their products to show up strategically on the big screen, but did you realize that advertisers have invaded schools, too? You may have heard of Channel One, the media service that delivers news and age-appropriate commercials directly to many classrooms and has sparked plenty of controversy in the process. But even schools that don't subscribe to Channel One still act as middle-men for advertisers, although it may be less obvious. We've seen pizza chains sponsoring reading contests, and frozen-food company ads on school lunch menus. Some soup and cereal companies encourage schools to redeem labels and box tops (by the truckload) for classroom equipment. The school, in turn, encourages you to buy those products.

After a lifetime of constant exposure to sophisticated advertising tactics, we are as well-trained as Pavlov's dogs: If they show us Product X enough times, we'll go buy it. Advertisers have it made. Unlike our grandparents, we hand over our hard-earned money without a fight.

If we sound a little jaded, it's because we are. After three years of staying home with our children, we realize that we could have been home much sooner if we hadn't bought into the great American "buy-it-because-it's-there" lifestyle, literally. Ironically, you probably couldn't tell by looking at us that we are any different from our working-parent counterparts. We do (and buy) many of the same things that they do, but we don't spend money thoughtlessly. When we quit work, money needed to go further. Necessities had to be sorted from luxuries. The difference between need and want had to become clearly defined.

Needs are goods or services that are essential to the following: nourishment, appropriate clothing, shelter, transportation, education, and good mental or physical health. We haven't given up all luxuries, but we don't consider buying everything that comes down the pike. What began as penny-pinching out of necessity has grown into a philosophy of practical frugality. At first, very careful money management allowed us to continue to stay home. As we began to get caught up—and then to get ahead—thoughtful spending had grown into a habit. Our philosophy is simple: *Whether you have a little or a lot, wasting your money makes no sense whatsoever.*

And when you do buy something...

When we see something we would like to buy, we've grown accustomed to asking ourselves questions before pulling out our wallets. The questions go something like this:

- ◆ Is this item a need or a want?
- ◆ Can I really afford it?
- ◆ Are there long-term ramifications associated with owning this thing?
- ◆ Do I own something now that does/can serve the same purpose?
- ◆ Is there something else I'd rather spend this amount of money on?
- ◆ Is this product *worth* the cost?

This thought process has become second nature for us, and we use it on both large and small purchases. All the questions are self-explanatory with the possible exception of the last one. Whether something is worth its price depends entirely on the buyer. How do you plan to use it? How often? How long do you expect it to last? What level of performance do you require from this thing? Are you willing to do the required maintenance on it? For your purposes, how does this particular product compare to its more or less expensive competitors? How important is owning this product to you? Only you can answer these questions. But because the concept is so abstract, we offer the following examples from our own households. Notice how the tally at the checkout is *not* necessarily the bottom line.

A tale of two shorts

Malia, formerly the poster child for expensive taste, bought a pair of designer khaki shorts for $54. They were well-constructed, classically styled, made of high-quality, substantial cotton, and went with absolutely everything. She loved them so much she wore them three or four times a week. And because she lives in a warm climate, she was able to wear them up to 10 months every year. They were easy to care for, too. She washed them in cold water, shook them out, and hung them to dry, with no ironing needed. After three years, they still looked like new.

When she saw some more khaki shorts on sale for $19.99, she bought them so she would always have a clean pair of khaki shorts. They were a department store's own brand, and weren't as well-made as the first shorts. Unfortunately, they needed ironing after washing and because of this, Malia wore them once a week at most. After one year, the cheap plastic zipper broke and since the shorts were usually a mass of wrinkles anyway, Malia didn't fix them. Two years later, the original khaki shorts finally began to fray. Malia wore them to wash the car or work in the yard until her second child was born and the shorts didn't fit anymore.

In the end, the designer shorts cost about 8 cents per wearing, and the inexpensive shorts cost about 50 cents per wearing. We have to conclude that, due to inferior quality, the inexpensive shorts weren't worth their cost. We realize that most people may not get this much use out of a pair of shorts, but for Malia the pricey shorts actually ended up being far cheaper, and were worth their cost.

The can-can

Neither of us buys many convenience foods, but we do keep canned soup in our pantries. We keep tomato soup for eating as is, and cream of chicken, mushroom, or celery for cooking. Through trial and error, we've discovered that our families will not eat the store-brand tomato soup available in our grocery store, because they don't like the flavor, or lack thereof. For us, it's worth paying national-brand prices for tomato soup that gets eaten, versus paying a dime less per can for tomato soup we end up feeding to the dog. On the other hand, the cream soups are always combined with other ingredients and cooked into a casserole. In our recipes, the taste difference between famous, brand-name cream soup and generic cream soup isn't noticeable. For cooking purposes, paying an extra dime for cream soup is definitely not worth it.

Dialing for dollars

Mary needed a telephone. She wanted a cordless phone so she could use it on the back porch, and she needed a durable phone because she has a teen-aged daughter. She went to her local warehouse store and was confronted with the following choices: a basic corded phone with one-year warranty for around $10; a famous-maker cordless phone with no added features and a one-year warranty for $29; or a famous-maker cordless phone equipped for caller-ID, speed-dialing, multiple channels, tons of other nifty things, and a five-year warranty. The third phone, originally priced at $119, was on sale for $59, and clearly a great deal at half-price.

Mary, who adores technical gadgets very nearly bought the half-price phone. Finally, she had to admit that what she really needed was a phone that would ring and allow her to hear—and be heard by—the person on the other end. The only other thing she really cared about was having a cordless phone. In the end, Mary paid full price for the $29 phone. The super deluxe phone was worth $59, but Mary ultimately decided that having such an amazing phone wasn't worth $59 to her.

And finally...

If the following tricks aren't already up your sleeve, they're worth developing.

Organization. We aren't super-organized, but we've found that even a little organization helps us make the most of our time, money, and energy. Keep a running grocery list on the fridge to cut down on little trips to the supermarket. Plan to run several errands at the same time. Keep up with the regular maintenance on your home and car. Make a list of household projects—washing windows, cleaning out closets, or whatever—and plan to tackle one each week. Put a calendar by the telephone and note all appointments or events for anyone in your family. Clear out household clutter, and don't allow more clutter to accumulate. Spend 10 minutes in the evening making lunches, helping the kids decide what to wear tomorrow, or just straightening up around the house. Before you go to bed, decide what you want to accomplish the next day so you'll know exactly where to start. Once you get organized it's fairly simple to stay organized, and life runs more smoothly.

Creativity. Don't confuse the definition of creativity with a talent for painting, sculpting, or making tacky souvenirs out of driftwood and seashells. Creativity is the ability to look at something—an object or situation—and see the potential for a new application or answer. Corporate America called this "paradigm shifting" 10 years ago, and now they call it "thinking outside the box," which is, of course, easier to spell. We especially like the term "thinking outside the box," because it's a wonderful metaphor for the creative process: Step outside the usual way of thinking in order to recognize a completely innovative solution. Whether you're still working or have just recently returned home, the ability to come up with innovative solutions to household or budgetary problems will be invaluable and make your life more enjoyable.

When Malia moved back to her hometown with her family, they decided to rent rather than buy a home right away. They rented a lovely two-bedroom house, which meant that Malia's daughters—Camille, 8, and Maggie, 1½—would have to share a bedroom. Camille was understandably nervous about her treasures being wrecked by a marauding toddler, and it quickly became clear that keeping the bedroom neat would be impossible.

After much rearranging and shuffling of stuff, Malia's husband, Tim, came up with a splendid (and very creative) idea. He went up into the unfinished attic and cleared out a large space by the window. He used old moving quilts for rugs, egg crates for book shelves, and rigged up some tiny white Christmas lights. He propped up some old pictures, hung some old posters from the rafters, and hauled up a footlocker full of dress-up clothes and an old mirror. A rock collection, seashells, art supplies, and board games followed later, along with a 1960s purple wicker chair from Malia's grandmother's garage.

It has turned out to be a fantastic solution. Camille and her friends can play without having to worry about Maggie getting hold of something she shouldn't, and no one has to deal with a cramped and messy bedroom. Tim had approached the problem from a completely new angle. No amount of reorganizing toys and rearranging bedroom furniture could have worked out so well.

Creativity is a skill. Like any other skill, you can learn it and get better with practice. Children are naturally creative because the world is still new to them. By the time we're adults, we've spent about 20 years learning the "correct" way to do all kinds of things.

Consider the way our educational system works: So much of what we learn in school is absolute. Light travels faster than sound. Proper nouns are always capitalized. The Magna Carta was signed in 1215. At school, answers are either right or wrong. Even the best schools are hard-pressed to give more than a token nod to creativity—and even then, creativity may be encouraged only in art class. As a result, many of us don't think of creativity as a tool we can use to solve everyday problems. If you suspect that your creative muscle could use some exercise, go to your library. There are plenty of books on creativity, and many of them offer activities or games that are designed to help you re-open your mind.

A good attitude. Of course, you already know that your attitude can color your experience, but we think the following axiom is worth repeating: *Never underestimate the power of a good attitude.*

Having said that, we know how tough it can be to maintain a sunny outlook, especially if you're working harder than usual to pay off some debt, or you're cooped up with rambunctious children through the third straight day of rain. Fortunately, you can usually think yourself into a better frame of mind. Here are some tricks we've used:

- ♦ Stop gritting your teeth and smile. Or hum. Or whistle while you work. Sometimes just pretending you have a good attitude is enough. At the very least, you might drive your co-workers or kids nuts, which is always fun.

- ♦ Take a minute to put things into proper perspective. For example, you might tell yourself: "All I have to do is stick to this depression-era budget for two more months, and then I will be off this ridiculous treadmill forever! What's 60 days compared to the rest of our lives?"

- ♦ When you're grumpy about having to do some chore that you hate, remind yourself that you could be doing something worse. Our personal favorite is: "As much as I despise ironing shirts, it's nowhere near as bad as sitting through yet another overlong, unproductive, blame-fest of a meeting. At least ironing gives me a chance to watch Oprah!"

- ♦ Count your blessings. This may sound corny, but do it anyway. If that doesn't work, watch the film version of *Pollyanna*. Your library may have it in the children's video section.

Remember your payoff

For us, the combination of a more frugal attitude, thoughtful consumerism, and the fact that we weren't actually bringing home much of our income, has made us financially better off than we ever we when we worked. It took a few months, but now we each enjoy a comfortable lifestyle, remain relatively calm most of the time, and raise our own children. Whatever your reasons for wanting to become a single-income family, keep them at the front of your mind at all times.

Chapter 5

Ready, Set, Go!

Beware of false expectations

When Ozzie came home from work, he was always smiling and genuinely happy to see the rest of the Nelson family. And it's no wonder. Harriet—always perfectly groomed and wearing heels and pearls, no less—met him at the door and ushered him into their perpetually tidy living room where he could read the newspaper. He could relax until Harriet served a delicious, well-balanced dinner (comprised of all the major food groups) in the dining room. Ozzie was never in a blind fury over something that had happened at work. Harriet was cool and composed. David and Ricky were always clean and decently dressed. We never saw a gigantic pile of Nelson laundry, or the Nelson kitchen ankle-deep in sporting equipment, or a week's worth of Nelson mail heaped on the kitchen table.

Want to know their secret? The television crews only showed up on the good days.

Obviously, neither you nor your spouse expects that life will become as perfect once one of you is managing the home and hearth. Life will be so much easier, but there will still be days when someone runs out of clean underwear or nights when dinner somehow takes an hour longer to cook than it should. Before you make the jump from two incomes to one, you need to discuss your expectations for your household and come to some meeting of the minds. Here are a few points to get the conversation started.

You can only accomplish so much in a day

This goes double for anyone who has children at preschool age. Don't be surprised if you aren't able to complete your "To-Do" list more than about two-thirds the time. With this in mind, you may want to decide on a few priorities.

For example, in our respective homes, eating dinner on time is a daily priority. If the living room looks like a bomb went off and there's only enough time to either start dinner or tidy the living room, we start dinner. But we know of another family who does the reverse. They have agreed that if it really comes down to a choice, they would rather have cornflakes for dinner and a clean living room. So, every once in a while, cornflakes it is.

Agree on the division of labor

We know a few stay-at-home moms who hardly do any housework at all. Since they quit work to take care of the children, they're of the opinion that taking care of the children is the single most important thing in the world, and that they shouldn't be expected to do the housework when the children are awake. They still expect their working spouses to do half the household chores. The dads in these homes apparently aren't thrilled with this arrangement, and we don't blame them. We also know a few men who have not lifted a finger to do anything around the house since their spouses quit working. The moms hate it because they feel like indentured servants, and we don't blame them, either.

It's clearly possible to handle the majority of the housework, even with small children—women have done this successfully throughout history. But it's not reasonable to demand that one person be solely responsible for a house, children, errands, cooking, yard work, automobiles, and everything else without help from anyone, ever. Don't assume that the two of you are automatically on the same wavelength about the division of labor. Decide together who will be in charge of what.

Agree to share budget responsibility

If you both set up a budget, but only one of you sticks to it, it won't work. Don't expect that neither of you will ever fall off the wagon, but you should both make a valiant effort to keep your finances in order. You may want to agree on how to handle windfalls and unexpected expenses. You may want to decide what dollar amount requires discussion before it's spent. (For example, you may agree to discuss whether to buy anything that costs more than $100.) At the very least, agree to be honest with each other about finances.

Respect each other's job and position

It's not always easy to go off to a job every day, nor is it always a picnic to run a household. Different roles come with different perks and pitfalls. Just as the parent at home doesn't want to feel like household help, the sole-bread winner of the household doesn't want to be regarded as a cash cow. Both of your jobs are vitally important to your family, and neither of you should ever forget it.

Stay-at-home myths shattered

♦ You will not have all the time in the world (even though it should seem otherwise).
♦ Daytime television is really not that great.
♦ When the kids are out of school, summers will seem twice as long.
♦ You will not magically begin to love housework.
♦ Laundry will not *ever* be fun.
♦ Cooking is not as easy as it looks on those cooking shows, but it is fun when you get it right.
♦ If you weren't the arts and crafts type before, you will not magically become the guru of great craft items.

Getting the kids on board

Lifestyle changes affect everyone in the family, so you should certainly prepare your children. If you will be operating within a sharply reduced budget for a few months and your children are old enough to notice, you should prepare them for this, too. Also remember that although babies will just go with the flow, preschoolers who have always spent their weekdays playing with other children their age may worry about missing their friends. This is understandable. After all, your 3-year-old who has always been in full-time day care spends more waking hours with the other 3-year-olds in his class than he spends with you. Consider establishing a regular play date with your child's day-care friends.

School-aged children will probably be relieved to come straight home after school instead of going to after-school care. At this age, kids can readily understand the trade-offs the family is making. They can see how spending a little less money means Mom can stay home with them. You may hear some grumbling out of kids who are accustomed to getting something every time they go near a store. That's okay. This is the ideal time to start teaching kids financial restraint. They can practice with their own allowance.

If you have teenagers and have been handing them money every time you turn around, they may not be so accepting of their reduced circumstances. In fact, they may be mortified. ("Whaddaya mean I have to buy my own gas?!") Consider letting your teenager find a part-time job. This can be anything from a regular gig after school and on the weekends to occasional baby-sitting or lawn mowing.

Be upfront with your kids about why you want one parent at home. This is a terrific chance to show your kids which things in life *you* value the most. And remember that whatever the ages of your children and however welcome being home with a parent may be, there will be a period of adjustment while everyone settles into a new routine.

The need for a contingency plan

We all know that awful things happen from time to time, typically when we least expect them. The furnace dies on New Year's Eve, or you discover that you need a new transmission two days before you leave on vacation. The very best contingency plan for nasty, expensive, surprises is a big, fat, savings account. Personally, we're still working on that. The very worst plan is to hope you'll be able to muddle through somehow. Rather than hoping that nothing unexpected ever comes up again, assume something could happen any time. And it probably will.

Since starting this book, we have each had what could only be described as a financial catastrophe. When Mary quit her job, she took out a home equity loan and started a home-based business. Mary's business experienced phenomenal growth, and the demands on her time were more than she was willing to give. Because she had yet to take any profit from the business, it was clear that the family could get along without the extra income the business would someday generate. Mary sold the business. This resulted in financial trouble when the buyer, who was paying in monthly installments, stopped paying for six months. Mary found herself completely unable to make the payments on her home equity loan.

Malia and her family fared no better. Six months after Malia quit work, her husband accepted a promotion in another state. They put their home on the market and moved from New York to South Carolina, where they leased a house while waiting for theirs to sell. One year later, they were still waiting, so they were still paying both a lease and a mortgage. Money was getting tighter and tighter and their youngest daughter was just a few weeks old. Putting her in day care so Malia could go back to work was simply out of the question. Finally, after 17 months on the market, the house in New York sold. Three weeks later, however, Malia's husband lost his job.

Although we both had enough money in savings to cover a one-time expense like replacing the refrigerator or having a major repair done on the car, paying ongoing living expenses out of savings would have wiped us out in no time. Luckily, when we first quit working we had thought a lot about what to do if we couldn't make ends meet. We knew that we had several options for coming up with money, short of begging for our old jobs back. When the unthinkable happened, we didn't waste time wringing our hands and trying to decide what to do. Instead, we were able to take specific, pre-planned, steps immediately to try and get the situation under control.

When sketching out a contingency plan, remember this: Your second income is netting you so little that, once you've stabilized your finances on one income, you will actually be in a better position to handle a financial crisis than when you both worked. This is because with both of you working full-time your options for making some extra money are very limited. However, if one of you is home, that person can arrange to pick up some temporary part-time employment if absolutely necessary. You'll also have more freedom to do a little creative problem-solving. Ultimately, you will have to decide for yourselves what is the most reasonable contingency plan for your family, but take some time to consider the alternatives. Here are some thoughts to get you started:

Tighten your belt even more. Even those of us on a budget could spend less money than we actually do, so it's possible to save money out of the monthly cash flow. For example, if your television needs repairs to the tune of $75, you could probably save $75 by really trimming the grocery bill for a month. The greater the expense, the more places you'll need to cut back.

Dip into your savings. What are savings accounts for, if not for a rainy day? If you don't have a savings account, put this book down, go open one immediately, and put *something* in it every month.

Put it on your credit card. What!? The same women who have been telling you for the last two chapters to be fiscally responsible are now blithely telling you to run up your credit card? Well—sort of. A credit card isn't a lifeline, but it's an extremely useful resource. If you have to make an emergency purchase you *can* put it on your credit card. We each keep one major credit card and, barring emergencies, we only use it for things we can pay completely pay off when the bill comes in. This way, if we do get into a jam, there is always plenty of credit available. Also, we have a maximum dollar figure that we are willing to put on the credit card that's actually far less than the limit on the card. We don't advise using your credit card to pay living expenses in any case. Use it for isolated expenses, and pay it off as soon as possible.

Seek temporary employment. If your financial crisis is larger than replacing the washing machine or having a new alternator put in your car, you might want to consider some form of temporary employment. Temporary work can be very helpful, if you can do it *without* incurring all the traditional work-related expenses. For a while, in addition to cutting our usual monthly spending, we both worked temporary part-time jobs. Mary spread the word in her community and was offered a position as a teacher's aide at her girls' school. For two months, she worked when school was in session, thereby dodging the need for after-school care.

Malia contacted the local office of the company she had worked for when she lived in New York. She explained her situation and suggested several things around the office that she would be able to do. As it turned out, the manager was happy to use Malia to help handle the busy office and work on backlogged projects. For a couple of months, Malia worked two or three days each week while her husband pursued his job hunt and took care of the baby. This left two or three days for him to interview each week while Malia was home.

The keys to locating temporary employment are to take the creative approach to finding work, and to be willing to do work that is outside your previous experience. You can always go to the temporary help agencies, but also remember to let as many people as possible know that you're looking to make some extra money; sometimes the best situations come to you through the grapevine. In addition to friends and relatives, you may want to contact your accountant, your hairdresser, your bank tellers, or anyone else who talks to other businesspeople during the course of the day. These are the people who will know what's going on in your local business community. Be honest about how much you're able to work, and be as flexible as you can. You may find one business that needs some extra help for a few weeks, or you may find three businesses that are willing to use someone half a day each week indefinitely.

Typically, temporary positions aren't the very best showcase for your considerable talents. Don't be afraid to call your former employer and explain your situation like Malia did, but don't be surprised if the company you used to run only wants some help greeting customers and answering phones. Even if you used to be in management, be willing to do filing. If you were a department store buyer in your former life, don't turn up your nose at being offered a stint in the gift-wrapping area. If you insist on your former level of position, you're unlikely to find any temporary position at all.

Make money from home. Depending on your skills and how much money you need, you may be able to earn money from home. However, unless you are anxious to take on the demands and risks of business ownership, we caution you to think twice before launching a full-blown, home-based business. (Remember Mary's experience?) Brainstorm a list of services you could offer. Some people use this approach as a way to make extra pocket money regularly. Once you settle on an idea (or two or three), decide how to reach your potential customers; fliers or an ad in the local classifieds may be in order. You might be willing to type term papers for local college students, tutor children in reading or math, or offer lessons in sewing, cooking, or a musical instrument. Vacationers frequently need someone to feed pets, water plants, and bring in mail and newspapers. You and the kids could make this your summertime job. Do you have a hobby or particular expertise that others might like to learn? Many community colleges offer noncredit, continuing education courses taught by qualified instructors who don't necessarily hold a degree. Take stock of your talents and abilities. The list of potential small jobs is endless.

Extra income ideas to do from home

- Tutor children in the area.
- Typing (offer to type term papers or reports to students at local high schools and colleges).
- Watering plants and collecting mail for business travelers.
- Baking for working moms (bake cookies, cakes, etc. for parties, schools functions, etc.).
- Grocery shopping for busy families (throw it in when you go shopping and deliver the goods to their home that afternoon).
- Walking dogs for working families, or dog sitting if you are even more adventurous.
- Teaching on the Internet (any special skills you may possess can be turned into hard dollars via many online services, such as American Online).
- Proofreading. (Good places to market your services might be your local newspaper or surrounding businesses who need the extra help.)

Take this job and...

Now you're ready to turn in a notice and dive into your new, sane, life. When you resign, do so gracefully—particularly if your contingency plan includes checking with your former employer for either temporary work or a future reference. Give the customary notice (two weeks in most cases, but some employers request a month), and try to refrain from doing the happy dance in your boss's office.

Chapter 6

Home Sweet Home

Congratulations! After a lot of planning and wrestling with your finances, you've quit your job and headed home for good. If you're excited, you should be. You've given yourself and your family a brand-new life and we can honestly say that we've never heard anyone say that they regret doing it. Your time now belongs to you and your family. The question is, how, exactly, are you going to spend it? Naturally, you will have to decide that for yourself, but don't be surprised if you can't find your groove right away. We had each been home a couple of months before we figured out what to do with ourselves.

It's not just an adventure, it's a job!

We've heard that some women who didn't work outside the home felt like second- or third-class citizens. We thought that following our own interests while still being good wives and mothers and running an efficient household was the best gig going. We knew that we would have to do mundane things—cleaning toilets leapt immediately to mind—but we had no intention of living a ho-hum life.

As it happened, though, our first few weeks at home were made up of shapeless days. The house got cleaned, of course, and the grocery shopping got done, but we wasted a lot of time wandering around while we tried to figure out what to do next. At first the freedom from the ultra-structured two-incomes-with-kids grind was soothing, but it didn't take long for us to feel utterly useless. When we worked, we completed dozens of tasks each day. At home, the day had just as many hours, but even though we were always doing something, we actually accomplished very little. Worse, we recognized the signs of brain atrophy, and a life of underachievement loomed. We knew that being home was what we wanted for ourselves and our families, but we had the nagging feeling that we were turning into slugs. Then we changed our approach to the whole thing:

We began treating running a household as if it were a new career. This gave us a sense of purpose and direction. Suddenly we had a job to do, and we wanted to do it well. And we realized another thing, too. After years of saying to ourselves at work, "If this were *my* company I would...," we now had the opportunity to run things our own way with no bosses and no red tape. We began to think of household operations as a small business, and realized that if we did it right, we could run a tight ship (that is, get done what needs to be done so we could concentrate on personal and family life) and maybe even show a profit (for example, put money into savings and investments). We aren't unpaid household help, we told ourselves. We are *In Charge.*

And if you ever update your resume...

After a few years as an at-home parent, you can add the following experience:

Head of Housekeeping	Purchasing Agent
Chief Operating Officer	Textiles Expert
Executive in Charge of Dishwashing	Head Chef
Manager of Human Resources	Secretary of Diplomacy
Chairman of Volunteer Activities	Referee
Facilities Manager	Dean of Student Affairs
In-house Medical Director	Arbiter
Superintendent of Safety	Logistical Strategist
Chauffeur	Interpreter
Child Development Director	Inventory Control Officer
Minister of Domestic Relations	Cash Flow Analyst
Executive Director of Acquisitions	General Consultant
Sanitation Engineer	Efficiency Expert
Director of Research and Development	

Weekly planning and agenda-setting

There are as many ideas of what constitutes good housekeeping as there are houses, and probably more. Some people require that their house be immaculate at all times, just in case *Architectural Digest* drops in for an impromptu photo shoot. Others are happy as long as the health department isn't threatening to condemn the place and everybody has a pair of clean underwear. Most people are somewhere in the middle. Whatever your personal convictions, you will benefit from formulating some sort of household plan. After you pinpoint what level of orderliness your family requires, you can start figuring out how to maintain it as efficiently as possible, thereby leaving you (and your family) with maximum free time.

How much you can accomplish in a day depends largely on how your time is structured. For example, if your children are in school and you have no regular weekday commitments, you will have the better part of every weekday to arrange as you see fit. On the other hand, if you have an infant, your productive time may be broken up into 15-minute or half-hour chunks throughout the day. At-home parents of school-aged children could conceivably manage to keep the household in peak condition most of the time. Parents of infants or toddlers may have to settle for reasonably organized, and even then some weeks will be better than others.

Ever notice that no matter how many closets you have, your stuff expands so that every closet is always completely full? The same is true for your time. If you allow all day to do household chores, they will take all day. If you allow an hour, you can still manage to get most everything done. We knew the household chores didn't have to take all of our time, and we wanted to minimize the time we devoted to them while still doing a good job. After all, we were determined to find some time to pursue our own interests without having to neglect home and family to do it. After some trial and error, we found a basic schedule that has served us well.

Get up and get dressed

Silly as it may sound, getting up and getting ourselves dressed as soon as possible has an enormous impact on how productive we are during the day. This doesn't mean hopping out of bed and into ratty sweats, either. This means getting a shower, doing whatever it is we do to our hair, putting on our makeup (albeit minimal), and putting on clothes decent enough to wear in public. There are two purposes for this, the first being purely psychological: If we *look* ready for our day to start, we *are* ready to start our day. Conversely, if we are still in our pajamas, we are only ready to lounge around and drink more coffee. The second purpose is logistical: If we are dressed and ready to go first thing, we can run an errand or two right after dropping the kids at school rather than having to come home and get dressed first. This saves us the trouble and time of getting back out sometime later.

First things first

Our goal is to get chores out of the way as early as possible so we have the largest possible chunk of time to devote to other pursuits. We subscribe to the "almost always clean and usually reasonably neat" school of housekeeping. We've found the only way to maintain this level is to set aside one morning each week to actually clean the house and a small amount of time every day to do daily upkeep. We chose Monday as our housecleaning day, because the house seems to accumulate the most dirt and clutter over the weekend. Monday housework takes about an hour and a half. Starting at about 8 a.m., we go through each room tidying everything. Then we vacuum, clean the bathrooms, wipe down counters and appliances in the kitchen, and mop. We're done by 9:30.

On either Thursday or Friday, the first thing we do is go to the grocery store. We find that shopping early in the morning has its benefits. The store is practically deserted, the sale meat bins offer the best selection, we aren't hungry (all the better to stick by our lists), and by going as soon as we drop off kids at school, we don't get the opportunity to procrastinate.

On either Tuesday or Wednesday—or, heaven forbid, both—we run errands, either as early as possible or while we are out picking up kids from school.

We also have two brief routines that we follow every weekday. As soon as we return from the early school/errand run, we go from room to room and tidy up. We sweep the kitchen floor if necessary or we might run around with a hand-held vacuum. We also check to see if

And you think vacuuming is a pain!

In the late 18th century, the household schedule was an institution. When your great-great-great grandmother got up in the morning, this is what she had to look forward to:

Monday, washing day. An all-day affair involving three large tubs of water, a fire, lye soap, a corrugated wash board, and a lot of aerobic activity. No need to go to the gym on washing day.

Tuesday, ironing day. Ever wonder why they call them *irons?* Because once upon a time they were made of—you guessed it— iron. Irons were put either in the fireplace or on a hot stove to heat. Then the lady of the house would spend all day Tuesday ironing the things that took her all day Monday to wash.

Wednesday, mending day. Back before there were malls, there was mending day. Between frequent wearing and washing of clothing, mending was a given. Adult clothes that could stand no more mending were often made over into children's clothes, infant's clothes, and eventually, quilts. That's the ultimate in recycling.

Thursday, odd-job day. Any job that didn't have its own day could be done on Thursday. With more than half the week devoted to clothing and linens, one can imagine that Thursdays were often hectic. Kitchen gardens had to be tended, foods preserved, cheese and butter made, etc.

Friday, cleaning day. Forget the vacuum! Carpets were dragged outside and beaten with wicker beaters. Floors were scrubbed with elbow grease. Beds had to be aired. Everything had to be dusted and furniture had to be polished. We doubt that our foremothers were ever thrilled that it was Friday.

Saturday, baking day. You didn't think the week was over yet, did you? On Saturdays, many housewives did all the family baking for the coming week. No bread machines, no nonstick pans, not even pie shells from your grocer's freezer.

Sunday, church day. You might think that Sunday sounds like a day of well-deserved rest until you realized that sermons sometimes lasted two or three hours—most of which was spent sitting ramrod-straight on a rock-hard pew.

any laundry needs to be tossed into the washer. Bingo! The house is in working order and we've spent no more than a half-hour doing it. Then, around 4:30 p.m., we do a 10-minute run through the house, putting things back where they belong. The kids have to help this time. After all, it's mostly their stuff all over the place. This way, the house never gets so bad that it's a huge job to clean up.

Other chores (folding clothes or ironing, watering plants, paying bills, making grocery lists, or whatever) can be done either right after the morning routine, or worked in whenever it's convenient.

The calendar

If you don't already have a wall calendar with enough space to write at least three things on each day, get one. Record the following things on you calendar: everybody's birthdays, all anniversaries you are expected to remember, appointments, school functions, ball games, ballet classes, school holidays, and anything else you have to do on a particular day. Hang it where it can be seen daily, preferably near the phone. Having all your obligations for the month recorded in one place will help you manage your time. It will also help you avoid over-extending yourself, which is a very real danger, especially once your name gets out on the volunteer circuit.

A word about self-discipline

We would love to report that we get everything done because we are loaded with self-discipline. Unfortunately, this just isn't true, which is why the schedules have been so important. We've found that it's very easy to sit around, nursing that fourth cup of coffee while the morning slips away. With an agenda—even if it is of our own making—it isn't so easy to goof off. (Of course, we still manage it from time to time.) The beauty of the schedule is that when everything gets taken care of, we enjoy the time we spend with our family, or even by ourselves, more.

Chapter 7

The (Occasional) Battle of the Stay~At~Home Blues

We weren't prepared for a case of the blues when we quit our jobs; we were euphoric. Our friends said, "What are you going to do all day?" or "You're used to being so busy, you'll get bored at home." We assured everyone that we would be plenty busy, and this has turned out to be true. We haven't been bored for more than five minutes in the last three years. But we hadn't been home more than a month or two when we discovered the real drawbacks of quitting work and staying home: Our friends were drifting away, and our kids had more opportunities to drive us bonkers.

Finding people like you

Many of our friendships began to dissolve shortly after we stopped working. At first we wondered why this was happening, but looking back, the reasons are clear. Most of our friends were people we had met on the job—either the job we just left, or a previous one. It's easy to make good friends at work. After all, you spend more time with your co-workers than you spend with anyone else. But these friendships are usually formed as a result of proximity and camaraderie rather than shared interests. When we talked to our old friends, the conversations were predictable. They would tell us the latest on Susie in accounting and her fling with John in management, but we couldn't care less. We would tell them how great it was to stay home, and they weren't interested. We had chosen separate paths, and didn't have much in common anymore. After a while, we had no one outside of our family to talk to. We adore our children and love being with them, but staying home all day with children as your only companions can turn you into a blithering idiot. After catching ourselves carrying on conversations with telephone solicitors, we realized we needed adult interaction.

If you're lucky, you already know people who stay home, or you have other home-based moms in your neighborhood. We didn't. Since childhood, we had always had built-in friendships: classmates at school, college roommates and dorm buddies, co-workers, or an occasional neighbor. This was the first time in our lives that we weren't part of some group. We knew we would have to go out to meet people like us, but this was harder than we thought it would be. We had to figure out where the people were.

If you need to find some new buddies, remember that many people find like-minded friends at their church or synagogue, but you don't have to stop there. Most public libraries have a regular story hour for small children, and the same moms (or dads) and kids tend to show up every week. The kids enjoy it, and you get out of the house. After a few weeks of regular attendance, it's easy to strike up a conversation with the other parents. If your children are too old for story time but you like to read, check with the librarian to see if the library sponsors adult book groups.

Another sure-fire way to meet parents who are home during the day is to become involved at your kids' school. The schools (public and private) are literally begging for volunteers. Being a volunteer has the added benefit of letting you see the school in action instead of just hearing your child's interpretation of what goes on.

And on the subject of school, check to see if your local community college offers continuing education classes. Most do, and these classes are geared toward non-degree-seeking adults. The tuition is cheap and the range of subjects is wide. You're likely to find courses offered on antiques, cooking, photography, drawing, gardening, computers, writing, and some topics you never even thought about before. You'll get intellectual stimulation, and you'll be in a class with other adults who share at least one of your interests. Also, many community centers offer adult education classes or even activities (often free, or for a nominal cost) geared toward families with children. You may find these listed in your local newspaper.

If you're looking for new friends, the trick is to get out of your house. People like you are out there somewhere, but they aren't coming to your door to invite you to join a group or take a class. Just think about activities you enjoy doing, and use them as avenues to find other people who share your interests.

Keeping the kids busy

Spending more time with our family—especially our children—is the premier reason most parents opt out of the work force. We all should remember, however, that our job is to transform our kids into self-sufficient members of the community. Plus, there are things we need to get done. The first lesson in self-sufficiency should be that the parent at home is not the full-time entertainment coordinator.

This is not to say that we don't play with our kids or take them places, because we do. It's just that we also expect them to entertain themselves. Children who have been in day care may need some remedial training in this area. Be patient, and remember that in day care the whole day is structured, and children go from one planned activity to another. Also, many children who have been in day care are apt to be clingy once they have a parent at their disposal. You can help your kids find something to do, or you can let them sit nearby and talk to you while you get your chores done, but don't let them hang on to you all day. You'll hate it, and it doesn't do them any good, either.

On the other hand, all children get righteously bored at some point. This is where having a few tricks up your sleeve can save your sanity. We keep a box with arts and crafts supplies, but the box stays out of sight until we need it, so its novelty doesn't wear off. The good art box contains crayons, colored pencils, scissors, glue, drawing paper, and construction paper. The *great* art box includes all those things plus beads culled from your old costume jewelry, seashells found at the beach, scraps of cardboard or poster board, fabric scraps, buttons cut off of old clothes, and anything useful you can remember to throw in the box instead of in the garbage.

Another idea is to have you child "help" you with something around the house. Tiny children can fold washcloths or dishtowels. (So what if you have to fold them again later? This keeps them happy and productive for a few minutes.) Children who are a little older can scrub potatoes for dinner, put laundry away, take care of a pet, or water outdoor plants. Older kids are hip to this trick and may not tell you they're bored if they think you will put them to work. Still, you'll be able to tell when they need something to do. At this age, your kids might enjoy more involved projects that require learning a new skill, like sewing, knitting, or refinishing scavenged furniture. (In Chapter 9, you will find more ideas for bored kids.) Sometimes even your brightest ideas will be met with disdain. Remember that boredom isn't life threatening. Also remember that every once in a while it's fun to let the housekeeping go and play under the sprinkler with the kids instead.

Top 10 signs that the kids need something constructive to do

1. Your 13-year-old has been watching *Barney* for five straight minutes.
2. They've synchronized their Giga Pets to the atomic clock.
3. Your 4-year-old worries that she's not getting enough fiber in her diet.
4. The cat's wearing cornrows.
5. They've made up names and complete biographies for the dust bunnies under the sofa.
6. Their imaginary friends have imaginary friends.
7. They know first-hand that there are 84,936 names in the phone book.
8. All the sock drawers are organized according to the spectrum.
9. Your toddler is giving the dog a "bath" with your brand-new bottle of perfume.
10. Your teenager has stood in front of the opened refrigerator so long she is beginning to show the first signs of frostbite.

Dig up your dreams

The best all-around antidote to the occasional blues is the realization that you now have the freedom not only to decide how you want to spend the rest of your life, but to start to make it happen. This goes for the working spouse, too. Do you want to return to work some day? Maybe you really wanted to go to law school, but never did. Or perhaps your new love is painting landscapes and you'd like to try your hand at being an artist.

If your children are very young, you will find that you have much more freedom once they start school. Take advantage of it. If you've always wanted to finish your degree, you can make time to start taking classes again. You will have more time to hone a talent or learn a new skill. Whatever it is, you have the ability to make it happen with a little thought and planning. We both always wanted to write, and now we're able to do it. We never had the chance while we were still working. The point is, you get to decide what to do with your future. We can't imagine a happier thought.

That's it?

Everyone's experience is unique, but most at-home parents we talked to never felt as if they left anything important behind when they quit working. We never did. In fact, we expected most things to be a lot harder than they actually were. Maybe this is because we were finally where we wanted to be—at home—and we checked all that working-mother guilt at the door. For us, the decision to stop working was exactly right, and if you're still reading this book, chances are it will turn out to be right for you, too. Is every day fabulous? Heck, no. Are we happy? We can honestly say that we have never been happier. Do we feel like we're sacrificing anything to stay home? Absolutely not. Our lifestyle is infinitely better than it was before. We pinched pennies for the first few months, but that's over. Our finances are actually stronger than they were when we worked, thanks to improved spending and saving habits. Would we do it all over again? You bet. Only we would do it a lot sooner.

Part Three

The Nitty Gritty: Home Economics

Chapter 8

Beyond Coupons: How to Feed Your Family for Less

The average two-income family has plenty of room in their grocery budget to streamline expenses and still eat very well. For many families the monthly food bill is a substantial expense, second only to housing. Luckily, it is also the easiest household expense to reduce immediately if necessary. Spending less money at the grocery store doesn't have to mean subsisting on beans and rice, or spending all your free time scouring the newspaper for coupons. But it may mean you have to re-think your cooking and shopping habits.

Cooking from scratch

America is hooked on prepackaged convenience foods. Every supermarket is filled with aisle upon aisle of boxed dinners, spice mixes in little packets, and frozen everything. There are four basic problems with prepackaged convenience food. First, whatever is in those little boxes has been processed into oblivion, and many of the nutrients are long gone. Also, processed foods are typically loaded with preservatives, artificial coloring, artificial flavoring, fillers, stabilizers, and heaven knows what else. In addition, these concoctions are much more expensive than the cost of their ingredients. And finally, a meal from a box obviously never tastes as good as the real thing.

On top of all of this, some of these foods aren't quite as convenient as the advertisers would have you believe. You could spend about 30 minutes making boxed Hamburger Helper, or you could spend about 30 minutes boiling a little pasta and tossing it with seasoned ground beef. You've got to boil the pasta and brown the meat either way. How much time do the manufacturers think it really takes to add tomato sauce and dried herbs?

However, if the term, "cooking from scratch," still strikes fear in your heart, you're not alone. You may envision hours spent chopping ingredients, and countertops littered with dozens of dirty pots and pans. Don't believe it. Cooking simple meals is easy once you learn a few basics, and dinner will no longer be limited to what you can find in the entree section of your grocer's freezer.

Whether you're an old pro in the kitchen or a rank amateur, the first thing you need is a good, comprehensive cookbook. (If you don't already own one, you'll find our favorites in the appendix.) If you're new to cooking be sure you have a cookbook that explains cooking terms and techniques. Illustrations are a plus. Cooking is a skill, and the same basics apply to both good home cooking and haute cuisine. Mastering the basics will go a long way toward helping you operate a cost-effective kitchen while feeding your family well. Once you have a feel for the fundamentals, you'll be able to tinker with recipes without having to feed too many of your experiments to the dog. At this point, you'll also discover that cooking a good meal for a hungry family can be more fun than you ever thought.

Staples

Staples are those basic ingredients that every cook should have in the pantry or refrigerator at all times. See the chart on pages 92 and 93 for a suggested list of staples. This isn't an exhaustive list because your pantry will reflect the food preferences of your household. For example, Tabasco sauce isn't on the list, but Malia's family uses it as frequently as salt and pepper. Other staples, such as flour, sugar, or salt, will be needed in virtually every kitchen.

If maintained correctly, your pantry will be the most useful kitchen resource you have. You will be able to throw together a dessert at a moment's notice, extend a family supper when unexpected company arrives just in time for dinner, or transform leftovers so that no one realizes they're eating last night's chicken or roast beef. If your pantry isn't well-stocked, for a few weeks you may need to devote part of your weekly grocery budget toward staples. Once you have all your staples available, you'll find cooking and meal-planning easier. You'll also cut down on those mid-week, budget-wrecking trips to the grocery store.

Keep a grocery list and a pencil, posted somewhere in your kitchen. Then announce the following house rule: Anyone who uses the last (or almost the last) of anything must add that item to the grocery list *that very minute.* You may need to post the rule on the refrigerator until everyone gets in the habit. It is the key to never running out of a staple in between grocery trips. There is nothing worse than getting halfway through oatmeal cookie dough only to find you have one teaspoon of oatmeal.

The art of the list

If your goal is to live within a budget, it doesn't pay to be a fly-by-the-seat-of-your-pants grocery shopper. If you guessed that we're going to insist that you never enter the grocery store without a list, you're right, of course. But first we're going to tell you how to make the perfect grocery list.

Step 1—Check the pantry. If you've trained your family correctly, this step may be unnecessary. Theoretically, every staple that's running low is already on the list you've posted. This is the foundation of your grocery list.

Step 2—Begin your menu plan. Take two minutes to look around and see if any food you already have is threatening to slip past its prime. Did your neighbor bring over eggplant from his garden? Then plan to cook eggplant parmesan before the eggplant goes mushy. Has the roast in your refrigerator freezer been there for a couple of months? Sounds like you'll probably be eating roast beef in some form this week. Allowing food to spoil is no different than burning money. Anything you need to cook this week will be the beginning of your menu plan.

Staples

Flour (plain and whole wheat, if you use it)
Cornmeal
Baking soda
Baking powder
Cornstarch
Salt
Herbs and spices (black pepper, red pepper, basil, thyme, oregano, rosemary, chili powder, parsley, bay leaves, cinnamon, nutmeg, cloves, garlic powder, and any other herbs or spices you use often)
Bouillon, chicken and beef
Onions
Garlic
Lemons
Worcestershire, barbecue, soy sauce, or others you use frequently
Wine for cooking (as opposed to "cooking wine")
Ketchup
Mayonnaise
Mustard (yellow and Dijon)
Pickles (whole and relish)
Cocoa
Vanilla extract
Sugar (granulated, confectioner's, and brown)
Honey
Corn syrup
Chocolate chips
Raisins
White vinegar (you may also want to keep wine, apple cider, or other flavored vinegar on hand)
Vegetable oil
Olive oil
Shortening
Oatmeal
Rice
Dried peas and beans
Pasta (macaroni, spaghetti, and any others your family eats regularly.)

Peanut butter
Jelly, jam, or preserves
Popcorn
Cold cereal
Coffee
Tea
Milk
Butter or margarine
Bread (possibly rolls or buns, too)
Crackers
Eggs
Cheese (cheddar and parmesan, at least)
A selection of canned goods including vegetables, soups, and tuna

---

Just by checking the refrigerator and freezer you may come up with a meal or two. Then you only have to come up with dinners for the balance of the week (or two weeks, or a month, depending on your shopping schedule). But before you go any further with your menu plan, you will need to do one thing—check the grocery store sale circulars.

Fun and games with supermarket sales

Gone are the days when every town had one supermarket. Now most towns large enough to warrant a speck in the atlas have at least two. Where there is more than one grocery store, there is competition. You learned all about competition in high school economics: Competition is good for the consumer because, among other things, it drives prices down.

However, because the average markup on groceries is relatively low, you might not see an across-the-board price difference from one store to the next. Instead, supermarkets play games with weekly sales, hoping to lure shoppers into their store. Only by comparing the various weekly sale circulars and shrugging off store loyalty can you fully benefit from the competition.

You'll get the most for your dollar by buying a particular store's loss leaders, which will be featured in the store's sale circular. Loss leaders are items offered at such a low price that the store actually loses money on them. Often these are items the grocery store expects many shoppers to buy. For example, ground beef is commonly sold as a loss leader, as are whole chickens or chicken breasts. You're likely to see things like eggs, orange juice, or bags of potatoes for either half the usual price, or as a buy-one-get-one-free deal. Typically, the ridiculously low price is good for one week, and the next week something else will be offered.

If the price of a particular item is very low, the store may limit the amount you can buy at one time or, especially in the case of meat, offer the low price only on family-sized packages. Some stores require that you have store card to get the sale price, so make it a point to have a card from every local supermarket that requires one. To maximize savings, be willing stock up on anything your family will use when it's offered at a loss leader price. Huge packages of chicken or ground beef can be easily divided into meal-sized portions and tossed in the freezer.

Each week shop at the store that offers the best deals on things you want to buy. Of course, if different stores are advertising different loss leaders that you want to take advantage of, you can always make a trip to each store. Be sure to note, however, whether a given price is good only with an additional minimum grocery purchase and plan accordingly.

Step 3—Plan for leftovers. Once you've identified the loss leaders you want to buy, jot down the meals you will make with them. Remember to include side dishes and vegetables as needed. At this point, you may have easily come up with three or four main dishes for family dinners. Before you go any further, take a look at your menu plan so far. You know how much your family usually eats. Do you expect to have leftovers from any of the dishes on the menu?

There's no way around it: Leftovers are a fact of life. Let's say that you plan to serve roast chicken early in the week, and you know that whenever you roast a chicken your family never finishes the whole thing. Instead of letting the chicken languish in the fridge and feeling guilty when you finally throw it out, plan a main dish for later in the week that calls for cooked chicken. Following are some recipes that use leftover chicken. Notice how none of the recipes say to reheat the chicken and serve it exactly the way you did last night. These recipes were selected because they bear no resemblance to two-day-old baked chicken. Rather, they are brand-new dishes.

The idea is to minimize food waste without eating the same dish over and over again, and to keep you from buying more food than you actually need. This cost-saving strategy is one that restaurants have used forever. A prime example is soup of the day. Next time you walk into a swanky restaurant and your waiter tells you that the soup du jour is shrimp bisque, rest assured that the chef showed up at work that morning to find that seven pounds of expensive shrimp that didn't sell in its previous incarnation last night.

Be creative with your own leftovers. Soups, quiches, omelets, casseroles, and salads are all terrific vehicles for any number of cooked vegetables, meats, rice, or noodles. Following is a cornucopia of ideas to get you started.

Serial chicken

A well-baked chicken is one of easiest and most elegant dinners we know of, and you can handle leftovers from it in many versatile ways. Whenever baked chicken appears on the menu plan, you can bet a meal based on cooked chicken will be on our tables a couple of nights later. The recipes below will get you started, and you can check your cookbooks for others.

Chicken-filled crepes

Don't let crepes intimidate you! They're nothing more than extremely thin pancakes and are really very simple to make. They're also cheap. Malia makes two batches at a time and freezes the extra batch between sheets of wax paper.

5 tbsp. butter
½ pound fresh mushrooms, sliced
¼ cup flour
1¼ milk, divided
½ cup chicken broth,
   or scant ½ cup chicken broth and
   one splash dry white wine

2 lightly beaten egg yolks
2 cups diced cooked chicken
Salt and fresh ground black
pepper, to taste
1 dozen crepes

Melt butter in a saucepan over medium heat. Add mushrooms and sauté for five minutes. Add flour and blend well. Slowly stir in 1 cup of the milk and cook for two minutes, stirring constantly. Add the broth and cook on medium low until thickened, stirring frequently. Beat 2 tablespoons of the hot sauce to the yolks and then stir the yolk mixture to the sauce. Cook for about one minute and remove from heat. Add salt and pepper to taste. Combine half the sauce with the chicken. Divide the chicken mixture among the crepes, roll the crepes, and place seam side down in a lightly greased casserole dish. Stir the remaining milk into the remaining sauce and pour over crepes. Bake at 350 degrees until crepes are heated through and sauce is bubbly. This recipe is good enough for a fancy dinner party!

Chicken shepherd's pie

½ bag frozen sliced carrots
½ bag frozen green beans
1 can condensed cream of chicken soup
1 tbsp. Worcestershire sauce
2 tbsp. parsley flakes

2 cups chopped cooked chicken
2 cups mashed potatoes
(left-over or instant)
2 eggs, slightly beaten

In a saucepan, bring 1/2 cup water to a boil and add carrots and green beans. Cover and simmer on low until vegetables are crisp and tender. Add the soup and the Worcestershire sauce, stirring to blend well. Cook for two minutes and then remove from heat. Spread chicken in the bottom of a casserole dish. Pour soup and vegetable mixture over chicken and set aside. Combine mashed potatoes, eggs, and parsley, mixing well. Spread the potato mixture over the casserole, making sure the topping completely covers the chicken and vegetables. (The potatoes should be touching the sides of the casserole dish all the way around so as to form a "seal" over everything else.) Bake in a 350-degree oven until the potatoes begin to brown, approximately 35 minutes.

Chicken noodle soup

2 cans chicken broth
2 cups water
½ bag frozen sliced carrots
1 cup chopped chicken
½ cup chopped celery

½ cup diced onion
2 tsp. celery seed
2 tbsp. parsley flakes
1 bag egg noodles

In a saucepan, sauté celery and onion in oil or butter. In large pot, combine chicken broth, water, and carrots. Cook until carrots are tender. Add celery and onion mixture, chopped chicken, celery seed, and parsley flakes to pot. Simmer 30 minutes. Bring soup to a boil. Put the egg noodles into the boiling mixture. Cook until noodles are tender. Serve with cornbread or crackers.

Step 4—Finishing your menu plan. Add any leftover-based meals to your meal plan. How many dinners do you have so far? If you still need a meal or two, decide what else you'd like to cook next week and add those to the menu. Alternately, you may want to decide on the last couple of meals after you've seen the supermarket's reduced meat bin. This is where the butcher puts all the meats with imminent "sell by" dates. Some days the bin is a treasure trove and some days there is nothing worth having.

Incidentally, this is a fantastic way to stock your freezer and a painless way to try out cuts of meat you don't typically buy. Keep in mind that inexpensive cuts of meat should be cooked slowly, but are often the most flavorful. Refer to a cookbook for preparation methods. (Note: We frequently buy meat marked "reduced for quick sale," and have never had a problem with it. However, we do make sure the packaging is intact and the meat looks fine. We also either plan to cook the meat that night, or freeze it until needed, even if it's only for a day or two.)

If all this menu planning sounds like a lot of time-consuming work, it's not. At first, it may take you a half-hour to complete, but before long it will become automatic and only take a few minutes. Once you have a plan, you can make the perfect grocery list by simply comparing the ingredients needed for your weekly menu to the food that is already in your kitchen. If you're planning chicken tetrazzini for Tuesday and have everything except chicken and mushrooms, then chicken and mushrooms go on the list.

Once your list is complete with regard to the week's dinners, add anything you need to get for breakfast lunches and snacks. Be careful here, though. Prepackaged and heavily processed foods have almost completely replaced home-prepared foods in the breakfast, lunch and snack categories. We don't begrudge anyone a box of breakfast cereal, but we would like to point out that you can produce scrambled eggs and toast in about seven minutes. (Note: As we write this, eggs have recently been exonerated by the health police. Like so many other foods, such as coffee, sugar, salt, beer, and wine, eggs fall in and out of favor.) Also, remember that cereal, eggs, and pancakes aren't the only things you can feed you family for breakfast. A peanut butter or grilled cheese sandwich with a glass of milk makes a fine breakfast, as does leftover quiche.

Stop! Don't throw out that broccoli!

Here are some ideas to help you transform leftovers of all kinds.

Steamed broccoli

Chop and bake broccoli in a quiche with one cup grated cheddar.

Here's a great universal quiche recipe: Spread meat, vegetables, and/or cheese filling over the bottom of an unbaked pie shell. Beat together 3 eggs, 1½ cups milk or half-and-half, salt and pepper, and other seasoning to taste. Pour over filling. Bake at 375 degrees until the center is set.

Or chop broccoli and combine with cooked pasta, tomato wedges, and Italian salad dressing. Serve chilled and topped with crumbled bacon.

Steak

Slice very thin and serve on crusty bread with leaf lettuce and horseradish mayonnaise. To make horseradish mayonnaise, combine three parts mayo with one part prepared horseradish.

Pot roast

Chop the meat (or shred with a fork) and stir into the leftover gravy. Serve over toast for an open-faced sandwich or as a topping for baked potatoes.

Green beans

Make green beans vinaigrette. Marinate cooked green beans in an oil-and-vinegar-type salad dressing. Serve chilled or at room temperature. This is also good using steamed cauliflower.

Chili

Reheat and serve over baked potatoes. Top each chili potato with two tablespoons of grated cheddar.

Also, pour chili into baking dish and top with cornbread batter. Bake at 400 degrees until cornbread is done.

Plain pasta

Warm an ovenproof bowl. Reheat noodles by briefly immersing in boiling water. Drain. Put the noodles in the warm bowl and toss with butter, grated parmesan cheese, salt, and pepper.

French bread

Make crostini. Slice bread in half-inch thick slices, and top each slice with a little finely chopped fresh tomato, a dash of basil, and a sprinkle of finely grated mozzarella or parmesan cheese. Place under the broiler until lightly browned.

Make homemade croutons by cutting the bread into 1-inch cubes and sautéing in olive oil with a clove of garlic, minced, until the croutons are crisp. Store in a tightly closed plastic bag or airtight container.

Ham

Bake in a quiche with 1 cup grated cheddar.

Or chop up ham and cheese and make an omelet. Serve with salad.

Scrambled eggs and bacon or sausage

Wrap 3 tablespoons of scrambled eggs, crumbled bacon or sausage, and a little grated cheese in a flour tortilla. Put each one in a freezer bag and microwave as needed for a quick, portable breakfast.

Mashed potatoes

Add a little butter or sour cream, crumbled bacon, and some grated cheese to the potatoes and mix well. Spread in a baking pan and top with more grated cheese. Bake at 375 degrees until the cheese is bubbly and the potatoes are beginning to brown on top. These are just like twice-baked potatoes without the skin.

Rice

Make fried rice. Sauté rice in a little olive oil with scallions and green peas. After about five minutes, stir in two beaten eggs, stirring briskly until eggs are cooked. The egg should be in tiny pieces. Season with soy sauce. This is a very tasty dish, but it will be even better if you can arrange to have leftover pork chops at the same time. Cut chops into half-inch cubes and add at the beginning.

Pancakes

If leftover pancakes are fairly thin, wrap them in a damp paper towel and reheat very briefly in the microwave. Spread with peanut butter and roll up. Terrific as an after-school snack. If they are too thick to roll without breaking, place pancakes in a single layer on a lightly greased cooking sheet. Place under the broiler just until warm, taking care not to let them burn. Spread with cream cheese or jam, or both. Cut into wedges. Kids love these.

Megamoney eaters: lunchbox food, snacks

Packing your child's lunch can cost quite a bit less than buying lunch from the school cafeteria, but not if you're sending tiny bags of chips and boxes of juice. If you're buying those prepacked lunches with the crackers and little circles of cheese, you would probably be better off—both financially and nutritionally—forking over a buck and a half for school lunch.

Think back to when your mom was packing a lunch for you. Your spread was likely to include a sandwich, some cookies, and a piece of fruit. Maybe you bought milk at school or had a thermos filled with lemonade from home. Think real food. We promise your kids won't suffer psychological damage if their lunches look more like something the Beaver would have eaten than something on a Saturday morning food commercial.

If your kids get sick of eating peanut butter and jelly sandwiches, you can always get more adventurous. Anything that's fairly portable and can be eaten with a minimum of mess is fair game. Next time you're cooking chicken, throw a couple of extra legs into the pan and send those for lunch. Fried, baked, or even barbecued drumsticks are all lunchtime hits. (Just send an extra napkin.) Crackers, cheese, and pepperoni make a good lunch, or you could send a small container of tuna or chicken salad to eat on the crackers, instead. For an easy change of pace, make sandwiches on a bun instead of sliced bread. Does your child have access to a microwave oven at school? Many school cafeterias now have microwaves for students to use, and this opens up a whole new realm of potential lunchbox fare. You can send leftover macaroni and cheese, spaghetti, soup, or anything that should be eaten hot.

When it comes to lunchbox add-ins, here's a good rule of thumb: If it's individually wrapped, it costs two or three times more than it should. Apples, grapes, and bananas are all standard lunchbox additions, as are cookies and muffins. If your child wants to take pudding, gelatin, or canned fruit, you can prepare these yourself much more cheaply than you can buy them in little cups. We found 4-ounce plastic containers at a dollar store for less than a dollar each, and bought five for each child. We spend a few minutes at the beginning of the week filling the little containers with fruit cocktail or chocolate pudding and stacking them in the fridge. When it's time to pack lunch, we just grab one. The containers paid for themselves in about two weeks. Instead of juice boxes, send a thermos of fruit juice or homemade lemonade.

Back at home, snack foods can really run up your grocery bill. Premium cookies and potato chips often cost more per pound than steak! Keep a bowl of fresh fruit in plain view to encourage healthy snacking. Also, try some of your supermarket-brand cookies. Ginger snaps are great, and the generic versions are inexpensive and usually quite good. See the chart on pages 102 and 103 for loads of inexpensive snack ideas.

A crash course in supermarket psychology

Marching into the store armed with a list may your best defense against overspending on groceries, but the battle doesn't end there. Supermarkets use psychological warfare to help you part with your money. Have you ever wondered why milk is in the farthest reaches of the store? Or why the bread is almost always as far away from the milk as possible? It's because the owners know you're likely to be in their store for bread and milk between shopping trips, and they want you to walk past the maximum amount of merchandise to reach them. They're hoping you'll pick up a few more things on the way. Checkout lanes are lined with candy because the store merchandisers know you'll be waiting there with your kids in tow. They also know the average child will beg for any treat in plain view. Notice how the candy racks are at kid's eye level. They're counting on your children to become so obnoxious that you give in and buy the candy. Following are some tactics for avoiding other common supermarket traps and becoming a more cost-conscious grocery shopper.

Shop with a calculator. A calculator can be especially useful if you're just beginning to stick to a grocery budget. With one in hand, you can keep a running total, making adjustments to your list as you go along. After several weeks of paying such close attention to your grocery bill, you may find that you can estimate your checkout total, but we suggest that you still carry the calculator with you.

Snacks can be real food, too

Use these ideas, along with some of your own, to help your family kick the processed snack habit.

Veggies and dip. Amazing but true: Children who turn up their noses at the thought of vegetables as snacks are the same kids who nearly polish off the crudités platter before your party guests arrive. If you know your kids will be starving soon, arrange a plate with carrot sticks, celery, cucumber spears, and a cup of ranch dressing. Leave it uncovered on the counter and don't say a word. It won't last until dinner.

Celery. A good holder for cream cheese, peanut butter, or humus.

Finger sandwiches. Make up a plate of peanut butter and jelly, cream cheese and olive, tuna salad, or your family's favorite sandwiches. Slice them into quarters.

Popcorn. If you've been eating the microwave kind, you'll have forgotten how good real popcorn tastes, and how much cheaper it is to buy! It doesn't take much longer to make than microwave popcorn, either. Toss hot popcorn with salt and butter or finely grated parmesan cheese.

Muffins. Make up a batch of your favorite muffins. When they're cool, put them in a large bag and store in the freezer. Single muffins will thaw in the microwave in about 20 seconds.

Baked apples. This is a good way to use up apples when you have too many. Peel, core, and arrange in a casserole dish. Put a pat of butter over the hole in each apple and sprinkle with cinnamon and brown sugar to taste. Bake at 350 degrees until soft, but not falling apart.

Cheese and crackers. This is an old favorite. To keep it interesting, try Swiss cheese on rye crackers, melted mozzarella on wheat crackers, or cream cheese on graham crackers.

Homemade cookies. Many kinds of cookie dough can be refrigerated or even frozen. If you keep dough on hand, older kids can bake homemade cookies (a dozen at a time) without any fuss.

Apples and... Slice apples and serve with slices of cheddar, or with peanut butter for dipping.

Pizza. Next time you make homemade pizza, wrap leftover slices individually in wax paper and put in a bag in the freezer. This way, pizza can be re-heated a slice at a time for snacks. Toasted English muffins or bagels make nifty little pizzas. Spoon seasoned tomato sauce on half a muffin or bagel and top with cheese. Place these under the broiler until cheese melts.

And to drink...

Homemade soda. Combine equal parts fruit juice and club soda. Try apple, cranberry, orange, or grapefruit.

Lemonade. Stir a little lemon juice (fresh or concentrate) into a glass of water. Add sugar to taste. For fizzy lemonade, substitute club soda or seltzer.

Your calculator comes in handy when you need to do a quick comparison of often-confusing unit pricing. As we've said before, once we were home for a few months and our finances came under control, budget restrictions began to ease. We no longer choose to stick to an exact monthly grocery budget, but rather aim to stay within an acceptable spending range. When spending creeps over the top of the acceptable range for a couple of weeks running, out comes the calculator and, for a week or two, we keep a running total again.

Grocery store managers hate to see people with calculators. Not only does keeping a running tally curb impulse buying, but shoppers who pay such close attention to spending set a "bad example" for other customers.

Shop the perimeter of the store. Once you're mainly cooking from scratch, you'll notice that the bulk of the things on your list are found along the walls. This is where the produce, meat, and dairy sections are, and all the prepackaged food is down the aisles. (So are most of your staples, so you can't skip the aisles altogether.) Pay attention as you cruise the perimeter, because this is also where some of the best buys can be found. In addition to the clearance bin in the meat section, you will often find reduced produce and bakery items.

Be prepared to hunt a bit for these unadvertised specials. Often they're simply piled in a grocery cart that's parked in an out-of-the-way spot. Keep an eye out for things that can be easily frozen. The selection will be limited in the produce department, but anything you find reduced in either the bakery or meat sections should freeze well.

Become acquainted with unit pricing. Unit pricing enables the shopper to make direct price comparisons on similar items that may be packaged differently. You'll find the unit price on the shelf, usually below the product. There will be a tag with the name of the product, its regular price, a bar code, a bunch of nonsensical numbers and letters, and the price-per-unit.

The price-per-unit may be in small print and will say something like 23.7 cents per ounce. If you're not in the habit of checking unit prices, you may be in for a surprise. You'll find that "economy" sizes are sometimes more expensive per ounce than smaller sizes of the same product. Occasionally, you'll find that some store brands are the same price ounce-for-ounce as national brands.

Unit pricing also saves you from falling for the shrunken package scam. This is where you look at the price of a premium product and it's the same price as the store brand. "Might as well get the good stuff," you think. If you check the unit price label, you may notice that the premium brand is much higher per ounce because the package is smaller, but not noticeably so. The worst offenders we've seen so far are makers of sugar and coffee. National-brand sugar is sometimes seen in 4- rather than 5-pound bags, and a pound of coffee is sometimes only 13 ounces.

As helpful as unit prices are, don't forget to watch out for psychological tricks supermarkets play with them. For example, if a particular item is on sale, the cost-per-unit may only be calculated for the regular price, leaving you to figure out the sale unit price yourself. (To figure the unit price, divide the price by the number of units in the package. "Unit" refers to ounces, pounds, grams, or other measure is used on the package. A one-pound loaf of bread on sale for $1.49, for instance, is 9.3 cents per ounce, or $1.49 divided by 16 ounces.)

Also, don't forget to make sure the products you are comparing have unit prices based on the same unit. One store we frequent has one brand of vegetable oil unit-priced on a per-ounce basis and a competing brand unit-priced on a per-quart basis. Finally, think about whether unit price is a valid comparison. For example, you might find apple juice concentrate is 9 cents per ounce while apple juice in juice boxes is 6.5 cents per ounce. Remember, though, that 1 ounce of the concentrate makes 4 ounces of apple juice. The actual comparison is 6.5 cents per ounce for boxed juice and 2.3 cents per ounce for the juice from concentrate that you mix yourself.

Shop high and low on the shelves. This is easy. Retailers put the most expensive options at eye level because that's the first place everyone looks.

Beware of end-of-the-aisle displays. Just because something is prominently displayed at the end of an aisle, doesn't mean that it's being offered at a lower price than normal. Grocery stores use this display space, known as the end cap, to boost the sale of a particular product, and it's very effective. Retailers know shoppers will assume that any item on an end display must be on sale, and they capitalize on it. Frequently, the price will be listed as "2 for $X," thereby taking the ruse a step further. Two of anything for a single price certainly sounds like a sale, and the retailer has encouraged shoppers to buy two of the products rather than one. Guess what? Shoppers *do* tend to buy two of any item priced as a "2 for $X." Do yourself a favor. Before you stock up on green beans displayed at "2 for $1.18," check around the corner to see if green beans are regularly 59 cents a can. If so, rest assured that green beans are $1.18 for two cans on any day, and you can wait to stockpile them until they're really on sale.

Pay attention. We can't list every tactic that grocery stores might employ to enhance sales, because the supermarket psychologists are forever coming up with new strategies. Never forget that it's the merchandiser's job to help you spend as much as possible. If you pay attention, however, you can catch on to your grocer's favorite tricks and avoid spending more money than necessary.

Coupon-clipping: Is it worth it?

If you polled a group of black-belt grocery shoppers, you would find that many of them would fall into one of two philosophical camps. In one camp, you have the avid couponers. In the other camp, you have those who believe that coupons are a waste of time, not to mention money. We fall somewhere in the middle.

Serious coupon users report impressive results: Many swear they save hundreds of dollars each year, and even get many grocery items for free or nearly free. They're able to do this by combining double- and triple-coupon deals with in-store sales and rebates. We occasionally luck into a fantastic coupon deal and are very happy about it, but we aren't hard-core coupon users. In order to get the results that the big-time couponers enjoy, you have to make couponing and rebating a hobby.

Hard-core enthusiasts spend a significant amount of time searching for coupons, trading coupons, hunting for rebate forms, filling out rebate forms, and store-hopping to get the best return on their efforts. We simply don't want to spend our spare time that way. Also, there aren't coupons available on most of the things we buy. The vast majority of food coupons are for prepared and processed foods, and we buy very few of those now. Of the few convenience foods we do buy, many are generics or store brands, which are often still less expensive than national brands with a coupon. Admittedly, we might have better luck if stores in our area offered to double or triple coupons regularly.

On the other hand, casual use of coupons is easy and convenient. Sunday newspapers include at least one insert with nothing but coupons, and it only takes a minute or two to flip through the whole thing. The coupons we use are usually for detergent or personal care products that we buy regularly. It seems silly not to take advantage of a price break, even if it's only for a quarter.

In the end, our advice on coupons is this: Use them to whatever extent works for you, but check to make sure you're really saving money. The only real danger is being lured into buying a product you wouldn't normally buy at all—30 cents off a $2.50 box of premium macaroni and cheese is no bargain if you normally do without boxed macaroni and cheese altogether.

The supermarket's not the only game in town

Depending on the size of your city, you may have shopping options beyond your neighborhood supermarket. Check your local yellow pages for the following types of stores.

Wholesale clubs. In the last few years, wholesale clubs have sprung up in suburban areas all over the country. These clubs usually require a small yearly membership fee, and sell a variety of merchandise, including food and paper products. The food selection isn't as wide as what you find in a supermarket, and much of the merchandise is packaged in bulk. Originally these stores offered memberships to businesses and sold goods at wholesale (or almost wholesale) prices. However, in recent years wholesale clubs have courted the average consumer, and have raised prices accordingly.

Some things may be more expensive than what you'll find in your grocery store, so compare carefully. Still, there are bargains to be had, and if you shop the wholesale club often or take advantage of good deals on items such as electronics, tires, car batteries, books, and clothing, you can easily save enough to cover the cost of the membership fee.

Consumer co-ops. A cooperative, or co-op, is an enterprise owned by individuals or companies that use its services. Co-ops come in many varieties. There are purchasing co-ops, marketing co-ops, housing co-ops, and service co-ops. Credit unions are cooperatives, your electric company may be a co-op, and many national trademarks, such as Sunkist, Ocean Spray, and Land O'Lakes, for example, are cooperative-owned.

Neighborhood food co-ops enjoyed wide popularity in the 1960s and 70s. Food co-ops are still around in many areas and are worth checking into. Each food co-op has its own rules and methods, but here's a general idea of how they work. To become a member you must pay a membership fee, and you may have to agree to work a certain number of hours periodically in the co-op itself. The co-op buys foods directly from farmers or other suppliers, and makes them available to its members. Some co-ops have a market where members can shop, and some simply divide the goods among its members on a weekly or monthly basis.

The benefits of a co-op are greatly reduced prices, and often much fresher food than what you find in the supermarket. The downside is you probably can't exist on what the co-op offers alone, because only certain foods will be available at any one time. If you belong to a co-op that divides its purchases among members, you'll have to take whatever you get. This may be great when what you get is beautiful fruit and vegetables and gallons of your favorite ice cream, but not so hot when you get is a bushel each of rutabagas and turnips.

Health food stores. Even small towns often have a health food store, and if you've never visited the one in your neighborhood, now is a good time. If you're not a granola-and-bean-sprouts kind of family, check it out anyway. You're bound to find something you already use, and some things cost much less than their supermarket counterparts.

You'll also find superior versions of staples such as honey and real maple syrup at fairly reasonable prices. (These may cost more than you're willing to pay for use as cooking staples, but used sparingly they're a real treat. Real maple syrup bears no resemblance to the corn syrup with imitation maple flavoring most of us buy, and natural wild honey has all the complexity of a good wine.) Our favorite thing about heath food stores is that they sell a large selection of staples such as flours, herbs, spices, and nuts in bulk at a fraction of supermarket prices.

Farmer's markets. One of the most worthwhile trends the 1990s has brought us is the widespread revival of the local farmer's market. The one in your area may be a weekly affair in a city park with booth after booth of fruits, vegetables, and crafts, or one of those semi-permanent roadside stands located a few miles outside of town. Depending on where you live, your local farmer's market may be open year-round, or only during the harvest season. Farmer's markets typically carry a wide variety of locally or regionally grown produce, and sometimes they carry premium imported fresh fruits and vegetables, too. Prices tend to be cheaper than what you see in the grocery store and the quality is much better, thus, making a trip out of the way well worth it.

Ethnic markets. If you live in an ethnically diverse area, you're probably lucky enough to have a variety of interesting markets nearby. Even if you're not very familiar with a particular ethnic cuisine, groceries that cater to a particular group are worth a visit. You may be shocked at how inexpensive some common staples are. You'll find treasures like 50-pound bags of rice and soy sauce by the gallon at Asian groceries. These markets often have great, cheap, cooking utensils, too. Italian markets carry an enormous array of pasta, the best imported tomato products, and prosciutto you can actually afford.

Gardening and preserving

Any discussion about eating well as economically as possible would be incomplete without a few words about growing your own fruits, vegetables, or herbs. If you have the space and the inclination, you can plant a vegetable garden or fruit trees in the backyard. If you have the inclination but don't have the physical space, many edibles will grow happily in the corner of a flowerbed, or even in containers on a sunny balcony. A couple of good-sized pots of basil, for instance, can yield enough leaves to keep you supplied with pesto sauce for months at a time.

If you're new to gardening, take the time to do some research before you spend a fortune on tools for digging up the backyard. No matter how idyllic it sounds, a garden takes work to make it productive and cost-effective. Many people enjoy gardening, but just as many loathe it. Start small.

You also need to know which crops grow well where you live, and how long it takes them to become productive. If you live in Miami and adore Granny Smith apples, it may take 10 years to get enough apples to make a single Waldorf salad, assuming you ever get any at all. Your county's agricultural extension agent (look in the blue pages of your phone book) can answer questions and may have literature available on crops and planting times. The extension service will also perform a soil analysis for a nominal fee.

If you do put in a backyard garden, consider planting enough to have extra produce to freeze, can, or dehydrate. There is something supremely satisfying about a pantry or freezer loaded with your own produce in the middle of winter. Again, do some research before you dive in. Different fruits and vegetables require different methods of preservation to make them safe and palatable. Also, keep in mind the cost and logistics involved with each method.

Canning requires an upfront investment for proper equipment, and you must be careful to produce a safe product. Storage, however, is easy and free, and requires nothing but space.

Freezing is simple and freezer bags are cheap, but you need a freezer and risk losing everything if the power goes out for an extended period of time. Also, running a freezer costs money.

Dehydration yields a product that takes up very little storage space. Drying can be done without a commercial dehydrator, but you tie up your oven for days on end. Also, the reconstituted foods may not be suitable for all uses.

If you do decide to try your hand at food preservation, your county extension agent can advise you on the most up-to-date safety methods for preventing food-borne illness. Also, in the appendix, we've listed several cookbooks devoted to preserving food. Whatever you do, don't just wing it. Follow current, USDA-approved methods. Canning, freezing, and dehydrating are all simple and can save you money, but only if you turn out a good product without making your family ill.

Chapter 9

Cheaper Kids

According to *American Demographics* magazine ("Kids in Stores," Paco Underhill, January, 1997), in the United States, children between the ages of 4 and 12 influence in excess of $165 billion in spending annually.

Clearly we spend an astonishing amount of money on our kids. Kids need certain things, of course. We want them to have the best of what they need, much of what they want, and maybe even the things we didn't have growing up. This is completely understandable, but do we really need to spend *that* much?

Is there any parent who hasn't been guilty of overspending on his children at some time? We all do it, and we do it for a variety of reasons. Poor spending habits and guilt top the list. Now that you have taken a serious look at taming your general spending habits, let's take a look at guilt.

You've probably seen surveys showing that parents buy things for their kids to make up for not spending enough time with them. These are usually parents whose children spend most of their waking lives in day care. Once you are home, those guilt purchases can stop cold because the cause itself has been dissolved. The other kind of guilt is more insidious. This is the guilt you carry, or your kids impose on you, because somebody else's kid has something your kid does not. Either way, the guilt has to go.

Your kids: consumers in training

In Chapter 4 we talked about developing a jaundiced eye toward unbridled consumerism. Help your children develop one as well. This will serve a dual purpose. It cuts out a lot of whining, and your children will be more likely to develop good spending habits before they become adults with credit cards.

Our kids are exposed to an enormous amount of advertising, much of it aimed directly at them. One estimate puts the number of television commercials viewed by children at 20,000 each year. There are also billboards, advertising in schools, and all the other tactics that marketers use to deliver the get-your-parents-to-buy-it-for-you message to children.

And then, of course, there's peer pressure. Remember that many of the conspicuous consumers in your neighborhood have children, too. These kids are easy to spot. They're the ones who have all the latest video games, bicycles with more gears than they can operate, all-terrain vehicles, and more toys than they can take care of or ever use. These are also the kids who brag incessantly about all the things their parents buy for them. It doesn't take a psychic, or a psychiatrist, to predict the sort of consumers these children will become.

One of the most important gifts you can give to your children is to help them develop financial restraint. With so much temptation to have more and more things, your kids will not become thoughtful consumers by chance. You have to spearhead the process. It's not enough to refuse to buy an endless stream of stuff—that's bound to backfire eventually. Kids need to learn that they don't *need* something just because somebody else has it. You have to begin by setting a good example and providing your children with opportunities to make their own spending decisions under your guidance. Following are a few ways to get started.

Turn off the TV

Shutting off the television is the fastest and most effective way to dramatically reduce the amount of advertising your children see. Limiting television for our kids and ourselves, is something that we began as soon as we quit working, and we've made it a permanent practice. Spending an excessive amount of time watching TV is a habit. Some experts call it an addiction. It may take two or three weeks to break away from the screen, but once you've done it, the results are profound. Not only do you see fewer of the commercials that cause the "I wants," but you will be forced to find more productive and creative ways to spend your time.

As luck would have it, kids who learn to be more resourceful are often less expensive to raise. Reading a book costs nothing if the book comes from the library, and playing in the backyard requires no expensive equipment. There is also evidence that children who don't watch television become better readers and do better in school. We aren't trying to suggest that we never turn the television on, because we do. We glance at the week's listings and pick out certain shows and specials we want to watch, and then try to remember to watch them. We still keep up with the news on TV, and of course we have a supply of movies on tape. But our TV sets aren't always on, and "vegging out" in front of the television is banned on school nights.

Teach kids the deceptive nature of advertising

Next time you see a McDonald's commercial, notice how fat, juicy, and loaded with all the fixings the Big Mac looks on TV. Have you ever ordered a Big Mac and seen it look anything like that? No. Instead, you get a run-of-the-mill burger that's at least 2 inches shorter than the one prepared by the food stylist for the ad. There's nothing wrong with the burger you bought, but it's not quite the same thing the ad seems to be selling. Take the time to teach your kids what the advertisers are doing. They are presenting their product in the most appealing way possible so as to entice the public to buy the product. They are not setting out to instruct anyone in realism.

Toy ads are some of the worst. We've seen ads for plush animals that appeared to walk, but it turned out that the child was supposed to drag the animal around with a plastic leash. We've also seen commercials showing children having a great time in the bathtub with some wonderful toy, but across the bottom of the screen in tiny letters is a disclaimer that says: "Immersion in water not recommended." Point out these discrepancies to your children, and help them understand that everything isn't always as it seems.

Take the kids shopping with you

As soon as your children are old enough to grasp basic number concepts, start teaching them about comparison shopping. While you probably don't want your kids to know about every dollar you spend, there's no reason not to show them how Brand X flour is more expensive than store brand flour, even though they are essentially the same product. If you buy medium-grade paper towels, you can explain how the cheaper product doesn't meet your family's needs, and therefore it's not a bargain. Once they can read, show them where to find the labels on food. There's no need to bother with formal training sessions. Just chat with you children as you shop.

Give your children an allowance

Kids are ready to learn about spending and budgeting long before they're ready to get a job, so many parents start giving their children a weekly allowance. Having an allowance is a terrific framework for learning about spending and short-term savings. You usually hear two different philosophies on allowances. Some parents tie the allowance to the completion of chores so that leaving chores undone means a docked allowance. Other parents give allowance outright and use other punishment for neglected chores. We fall into the second group because we think kids should do certain chores just because they're members of the household.

However, we do give our children the opportunity to earn extra money (under certain circumstances) by doing extra jobs around the house or yard. If you decide to give your kids an allowance, here's a plan to get you started:

Decide what purchases will have to come out of the allowance and set the amount accordingly. Small kids will need enough allowance to buy a sweet or a small toy from time to time, so a dollar or two per week is probably sufficient. As children get older, you want them to have enough money to buy something small during the week, but not so much that they can buy anything that strikes their fancy. A child should have to save some part of the allowance for a few weeks before he or she can afford to buy something more substantial, like a video game cartridge or designer jeans. Giving children a small raise each birthday is common.

Establish the rules. Once you've formulated the allowance plan, explain it in detail to your kids. They should know what day of the week allowance will be paid, what chores will earn extra money, or the exact amount deducted for each forgotten chore.

Be consistent. Don't bend the rules and don't make your kids have to remind you to pay up. Remember, when you give your kids an allowance you aren't doing them a favor. You're teaching them responsibility and money management.

Jobs for kids

Hiring your kids is a good way for them to earn extra money, and a great way for you to get a few extra things done around the house. Here are some things your kids can do:

♦ Clean the inside of the car.
♦ Wash baseboards.
♦ Rake leaves.
♦ Wash windows.
♦ Polish furniture.
♦ Dust and tidy bookshelves.
♦ Straighten the linen closet.
♦ Polish silver.
♦ Vacuum under the sofa cushions.
♦ Fold laundry.
♦ Bathe the dog.
♦ Weed the flowerbed.
♦ Sweep the driveway and front walk.
♦ Play with younger siblings while you get something else done.

Don't dictate how the money is spent. You probably won't be able to keep from making the occasional suggestion, but spending decisions should be made by your child. Of course, if you've told your child that he or she isn't allowed to have something—a BB gun, for instance, or a pet snake—that's a different issue.

If they make a mistake, don't bail them out. If your 10-year-old spends all his allowance on candy and chips, and then doesn't have any money to buy something he sees three days later, he's out of luck. The only way kids learn not to blow all their money is to blow it all once or twice, and miss out on something better as a result. You may agree to an advance under very special circumstances, but don't extend credit routinely. A better idea is to have the child earn the extra money he needs by doing chores that are above and beyond the call of duty.

Outfitting the kids

Kids grow so fast that keeping them in clothes and shoes that fit is a constant battle. It's bad enough when they're little and don't care what they're wearing, but as they get older you're faced with a new set of horrors. Everything your kid wears will have to pass the "cool" test. In order to keep your kids dressed acceptably without going completely broke, you'll need to know a few tricks.

Playclothes

When did playclothes go out of fashion? When we were growing up, we always had playclothes, and so did everyone else we knew. We came home from school, took off our school clothes, and put on something grubby enough for climbing trees. If we slipped in the mud or had to put the chain back on our bike, it was no big deal because we couldn't ruin playclothes—they were pretty far gone in the first place. Playclothes were just regular pants, shirts, or shorts that had become so stained or faded that they weren't fit for wearing to school. The first key to saving money on kids' clothes is to make the ones they have last longer, and bringing back playclothes is a big help.

Finding good clothes for less money

During the growing years, you can expect to replenish each child's wardrobe at least two times each year. If you're paying top dollar for your kid's wardrobe, your clothing bill may rival your mortgage. Some of the following strategies can help you keep clothing costs in line. Incidentally, many of these ideas can be used to lower Mom's and Dad's clothing expenses, too.

Hand-me-downs. Also known as "going shopping in the attic." This is a trick that everyone knows, and it's a no-brainer if you have two or more children of the same sex. But even if you have both boys and girls, you can still use some things as hand-me-downs if you're a smart shopper, especially when your children are small. Plan for hand-me-downs by buying some unisex basics like T-shirts, plain turtlenecks in basic colors (white, red, navy, yellow, and green), undecorated jackets in basic fabrics (like denim or corduroy), plain denim overalls, plain sweatsuits, and blue jeans.

Yard sales. Some people have spectacular luck shopping yard sales and finding perfectly good clothing for children that costs practically nothing. If you look, you can find good deals on clothing for children of any age, but some of the very best finds are baby clothes. Check you local paper during yard sale season, plan your route, and set out early. The biggest drawback to shopping yard sales for clothes is the hit-or-miss factor. You may have to visit as many as 10 or 12 sales that advertise children's clothing before finding one that offers the sizes you're looking for. Thrift stores usually offer slightly higher prices than what you find at yard sales, but the quality and selection of clothing is similar. You'll see some great things and a lot of junk. Look in the yellow pages to locate thrift stores in your area, and if you find one you like, check in frequently.

Consignment shops. Don't confuse consignment shops with thrift stores—they're completely different animals. You'll pay more for good, used clothes in a consignment store, but the inventory is more consistent and the quality is usually high. This is because these shops are picky; they will only accept clothes in very good condition. The items you find in a consignment shop will be clean, pressed, up-to-date, not too worn or faded, and will have working zippers and no missing buttons. You can also take your children's outgrown clothes to the consignment shop and sell them for either cash or store credit.

Sewing. Sewing is quickly becoming a lost art. This is too bad because kids clothes can be easy and inexpensive to sew, if you know what you're doing. If you don't know what you're doing but want to learn, children's shirts, jumpers, or playsuits are good projects for beginners. Get the most for your money by buying patterns and fabrics on sale. Fabric stores run seasonal sales the same way department stores do, and frequently have sale tables with fabrics, patterns, and notions marked down to half-price or less.

Baby paraphernalia

Walking through one of the baby megastores at the mall would give anyone the idea that babies are horribly expensive to maintain—but it's not true. Babies need love, nourishment, diapers, appropriate clothing, a safe place to sleep, and more love. If babies needed a quarter of the things the baby industry wants us to think they do, hardly anyone would be able to afford them! Following is a list of overrated baby equipment followed by a few items that are genuinely useful. Remember that it's easy to find used baby gear in excellent condition, and you may even be able to borrow some things from friends.

Diaper Genies. Unless you leave garbage in the house long enough to cause a stink, these are unnecessary.

Changing tables. By far, the safest place to change a baby is on the floor. If you don't want to get down on the floor, change the baby on a bed or sofa.

Wipe warmers. You can warm a cold baby wipe by holding it in your hand for a minute. Your body heat will do the job for free.

Bathtub ring seats. During baths, let your baby sit in a plastic mesh laundry basket. Actually, this works much better than the ring seats because toys can't float out of reach and you can use the basket to store tub toys after bath time. Also, the ring seats can be dangerous if a baby slips and gets caught in the seat. And the suction cups on the bottom hardly ever work properly.

Electric bottle warmers. Fill a saucepan or deep bowl with your hottest tap water and stand the bottle in it. In two minutes you should have a wrist-temperature bottle. (Shake the bottle a couple of times while it's warming.)

Video baby monitors. Nothing beats actually walking into the baby's room. Nothing beats actually walking into the nursery to check on the baby.

Sheet savers. These are the quilted pads you put under the baby's head so if he or she spits up, you don't have to change the crib sheet. Before these were invented, people used a clean cloth diaper (folded in half) for the exact same purpose. You could also use an extra receiving blanket. You'll probably get scores of them as gifts.

Baby powder. Your pediatrician will agree: Babies don't need to be powdered down. If you simply can't stand not powdering your baby, grab the cornstarch out of the kitchen and use that in place of talcum powder. It's easier on the baby's lungs.

Toddler beds. What's the point? Your child will need a regular bed in a year or two, anyway.

Expensive nursery decor. Decorator nurseries with matching accessories are for parents. Babies don't care. By the time children do care (at about 2 or 3 years old), they'll be ready for a kid's room instead of a nursery. Save your money or buy things that will survive the transition.

Baby things that do make sense:

Baby swing. We've never heard of a baby who didn't tolerate being in the swing for at least a few minutes. Putting your baby in the swing will buy you enough time to take a shower or cook dinner.

Cloth diapers. Even if you use disposable diapers exclusively, cloth diapers are virtually indispensable as burp cloths. Also, many parents find that using cloth diapers for a few days often clears up a bad case of diaper rash.

Umbrella stroller. By the time your baby can sit up, you'll be sick of lugging around a 25-pound, high-tech, convertible stroller. An umbrella stroller is so much more portable and easier to unfold, that you may never use the fancy one again. Try to borrow the $100 big stroller, but buy the $20 umbrella version.

Extra waterproof mattress pads. You need enough to keep two layers of bedding on your crib mattress all the time. Put one waterproof pad on the bare mattress, then a crib sheet, then another waterproof pad, then another crib sheet. When your baby has a big spit-up or a diaper leak in the middle of the night, you can strip off the top sheet and pad, revealing the clean layer. This saves you from having to turn on the lights and completely waking up both yourself and the baby.

Portable playpen that doubles as a portable crib. Though usually you may prefer for your baby to be free, there will be times when you absolutely need to confine your baby in a safe place other than the crib. Even after your baby is too big to play in the playpen, you can still use it as a portable crib when you're away from home.

Off-season shopping. Shopping department stores at the end of the season is the easiest and cheapest way to buy new, famous-maker clothes for your child. It's not unusual to find bathing suits and shorts for just a few dollars in September, or coats and sweaters marked down 75 percent in May. The downside to shopping at the end of the season is that you will have to guess what size your child will be wearing next year.

Clothing swaps. A clothing swap isn't a place to go: It's an event you organize. Find several families with children similar in age to your own, and plan to meet twice a year to swap outgrown clothes. Participating families can take turns hosting the meeting. You may want to establish some guidelines similar to what consignment shops require (for example, no torn, dirty, or hopelessly outdated clothes).

The swap can be as casual or as structured as you wish. One method is to stack the clothes on a table and let everyone take whatever they can use. A more democratic method would be to establish a point system where families earn points based on how many items they bring to the meeting, and can then spend their points buying clothing from the swap table. If you include just a few families, the swap will be simple to organize. If you invite more families, you'll spend more time on organization, but the swap will offer a larger selection.

Toys and other kid stuff

The experts tell us that playing is crucial to a child's physical, emotional, social, and intellectual development. What kids don't need is more toys than they can play with, or toys that require no imagination. Before you shop, look at the toys your child already owns. Which ones get the most use? It's not unusual for children to beg and plead for a particular toy and then rarely touch it once they get it. Once you identify the things your children play with the most, figure out what it is about a particular plaything that makes it so wonderful to your kids. If you know why the well-used toys are so appealing to your kids, you can make better toy purchases in the future.

Off-season shopping

Toys go on sale just like everything else, and toy sales are pretty predictable. Large toy and discount stores often run big sales during the down time that comes just before the Christmas buying frenzy. After the holidays, stores mark down all the leftovers. If you can stand the crowds—and if you have any money left—this is a fantastic time to buy a few basics for gifts during the year, or even to get a head start on next year's holiday shopping. (We don't advise trying to buy everything too early in the year, however. You'll end up spending more money when something you never would have thought of turns up on your child's wish list.) When you're shopping those great after-Christmas sales, remember to stock up on small toys and books that your kids can give as birthday party gifts.

Yard sales and rummage sales

Although many of the toys you see at yard and rummage sales are downright battered, there are still some fantastic deals out there. You'll have the most consistent luck finding replacement pieces (like a box full of miscellaneous Legos or a bag of Barbie accessories), or children's books. You're also likely to see more expensive items, such as go-carts, playhouses, basketball goals, dollhouses, free-standing play kitchens, ski equipment, stereo equipment, high-tech bicycles, and good, child-sized furniture—all at a fraction of the original cost. Some things you find will need cleaning up, but many will look like they've never been used.

Toys for the imagination

Remember your dismay the first time your child opened a present, set the gift aside, and played for hours with the box it came in? Some of the best playthings aren't found in a toy store, but around your house or in your garage. A wooden spoon and a saucepan will delight any baby, and a cardboard appliance box is a terrible thing to waste. And don't forget to keep your eyes out for dress-up clothes for those wonderful, free-wheeling, make-believe games kids play. Collect a variety of hats, sports uniforms, shoes, jewelry, and other accessories, some of which you may find in Grandpa and Grandma's attic. Be on the look out at thrift stores and garage sales for things like tents, a Halloween costume, mismatched-but-fancy china cups and saucers for playing house, and anything else that looks both safe and fun.

The real thing

Next time your child asks for a toy version of something, consider buying the real thing (if appropriate), instead. For example, if your child asks for a tent to play in, don't automatically get a toy, plastic pop-together tent before pricing small, low-tech, real tents at a discount store. You may pay a little more, but a real pop-up tent will be sturdier. Your child won't grow out of a real tent, making it a better investment in the long run. Many kid-versions of real things are either so flimsy or limited in their use as to be almost worthless. A 12-year-old child who is interested in learning to sew is just as capable of handling an inexpensive adult sewing machine as a $30 child's model. A real machine is far more versatile, and can be repaired or adjusted as necessary. Plus, it can be used for many years, even into adulthood. Think "real but basic" when kids want items like tool sets, walkie-talkies, radios, cooking sets, and the like.

Dirt-cheap ideas for restless kids

Kids need fun places to go and new things to do. The good news is that having fun can be cheap, or even free.

Places to go

The public library. If you haven't been using your public library, you don't know what you've been missing. In addition to books, you can often borrow video games, movies and specials on videotape, audio books, music CDs, and toys. Most libraries offer activities for children of all ages, such as story hours and arts and crafts programs. In the summer your library might offer reading programs and contests. Some libraries even show classic movies for free.

Parks. Almost everyone lives within a short drive of a city, state, or national park. City parks often have playground equipment and a picnic site, and they are usually free. State and national parks may charge an entrance fee, but may have lots of things to do and places to go, including beaches, lakes, hiking trails, mini-zoos, and museums. Pack a lunch and spend the day.

Local events. Depending on where you live, various organizations may sponsor all sorts of events like free classes, free movies, art shows, lectures, demonstrations, and concerts. To find out about these happenings, look for fliers posted around town and check your local paper.

Fun crafts and projects

Decorated picture frames. For this project, you'll need at least one cheap picture frame and lots of little objects to glue all over it. You can use macaroni, pebbles, buttons, fake jewels, small seashells, pieces of old jigsaw puzzles, or anything else that can be glued to the frame. Decorated frames usually look best if the original frame is completely covered. Add a picture of your child and you have a terrific gift for a grandparent.

Rehabilitated furniture. Older kids might enjoy refinishing old furniture, especially if the completed project can go in their room. Take an old, beat-up piece of wooden furniture and let them at it with sandpaper and paint. Using contrasting colors is neat, and splatter painting, thumbprint dots, sponge prints, or freehand designs are fun to do.

Handmade books. Let kids make up a story or write their own version of an old favorite. This project is good for either the nursery-school set or grade-school children—the only difference is *your* level of involvement. You will need paper, writing implements, and something of thicker texture for the cover. For the little ones, you may have to take dictation, but they can illustrate their story. For bigger kids gather the supplies and let them get to work. When the pages are finished, help them fashion a cover for their creation. You can use fabric scraps or cardboard secured with staples, or "bind" it with string threaded through punched holes.

Paperweights. Everybody needs a few paperweights! They can be made from rocks, chunks of wood, or anything else heavy enough to hold paper down. Set the kids up with the paperweights-to-be and several colors of paint. This can be done outdoors, but if it's a rainy-day project, spread newspapers on the table and an old sheet on the floor. Dad's ratty old dress shirts make good painter's smocks.

Very versatile buttons. Remember playing in your grandmother's button box when you were small? We don't know why buttons are so much fun, but they are. Old buttons can be used for countless craft projects, and small children can string them using a large, blunt needle and yarn. Children can sort buttons by color, size, or type. To build your button collection, make sure to harvest any buttons from discarded clothing too worn to donate to a charity.

Wrapping paper. This is a dual-purpose activity. It keeps kids busy on bad-weather days, and allows you to accumulate a supply of one-of-a-kind gift wrap. The paper can be butcher paper, brown wrapping paper (for shipping boxes through the mail), or newsprint end rolls. (End rolls are the leftovers from a roll of newsprint that are too measly for the newspaper to bother using up. These rolls are often 100 feet long or longer. Contact your local newspaper. Some papers sell end rolls for a couple of dollars each, or even give them away.) Spread your wrap out on a long table and let kids make painted designs with sponges, potato stamps, or even their hands. Let the paint dry completely before you roll it back up. Store in a dry place and use like any other wrapping paper.

Place mats. These are fun to make, fun to use, and could even make nifty homemade party favors for a birthday party. To make place mats, have your children decorate a piece of construction paper. They can make a collage, a drawing, a glitter design or anything else that will lie flat. To make the place mat spill-proof, cover the whole picture, front and back, with clear contact paper. Trim the edges, and *presto!*, you have a place mat!

Ocean in a bottle. This is a good, dead-of-winter diversion. You will need a clear plastic bottle, tap water, food coloring, oil (baby, mineral, or vegetable oils all work fine), and some glue. Fill the bottle about halfway with water tinted blue or blue-green. Add oil, leaving a 2-inch space at the top of the bottle. Cap the bottle and run a bead of glue around the edge of the cap to prevent leaks. Moving the bottle will produce realistic-looking waves. For added interest, you can put small plastic fish or tiny seashells in the bottle, too.

Birthday parties on a budget

When we were little, a birthday party meant dressing nice and going to a child's home for cake, ice cream, and a couple of rounds of "pin the tail on the donkey." After games and cake, there were small gifts for the birthday child, and then everyone's parents arrived to pick them up. Everybody had a pretty good time and the whole thing lasted about two hours. Kids turning 11 or 12 might have a sleepover with two or three friends.

Today's birthday parties are nothing like that. Now parties are *events* hosted at an indoor playground, the local skating rink, or amusement park. We've even seen it go as far as 8-year-old girls getting picked up in a limo and delivered to the party. Birthday parties have moved into the competitive arena. We think it's high time to reverse this trend.

The best parties are simple and kid-friendly. Remember that half the fun for your child is the planning and preparation, so let the birthday boy or girl have a hand in choosing invitations, party favors, and decorations. Here are some rules of thumb:

♦ It's a good idea to limit the number of guests to your child's age. For example, a child turning six can invite six friends to his party.

♦ Party supply stores have sprung up across the country, and they offer a huge selection of favors, decorations, and paper plates and cups for reasonable prices.

♦ Games are great, but don't offer prizes unless everybody gets one.

♦ Always list a specific beginning and end time on the invitation.

Kids adore theme parties, and they're the most fun to plan and create. To get you started, we've included a list of some of the best theme parties we've seen.

The cooking party

This kind of party is different, fun, and easily adaptable for most age groups. The party is held in the kitchen with Mom or Dad as the head chef. The kids will actually make the party food and then sit down to their feast. Small kids should work with partially prepared food. They can top individual pizzas, decorate cupcakes, and help churn homemade ice cream. Older kids can do more actual cooking, with groups of two or three working on a particular dish. This is hilarious to watch! Keep plenty of towels handy and forget about the counters and the floor for a few hours.

Invitation ideas
♦ Wooden spoons with tags attached.
♦ Cards cut in the shape of a chef's hat.
♦ Hand-lettering on a small paper plate.

Menu ideas
For young children:
♦ Individual pizzas the kids top themselves.
♦ Cupcakes for kids to decorate.
♦ Ice cream.

For older kids:
♦ Lasagna (start the sauce ahead of time and let them "build" it).
♦ Salad.
♦ Parfaits made with cubes of pound cake, ice cream, fruit, dessert sauce, and whipped cream.
♦ Do-it-yourself sundaes served on a brownie.

Game ideas
♦ Pin the hat on the chef.
♦ Messiest apron award.
♦ Cleanest apron award.

Party favors
♦ An apron (get them cheap at a restaurant-supply store and use fabric paint pens to personalize each one).
♦ Paper chef's hat (also available in restaurant supply stores).
♦ A small recipe book (include the recipes for the party food).

Prizes
♦ Cooking tongs.
♦ An oven mitt or pot holder.
♦ Medals made from decorated cardboard circles and hung around the child's neck with a ribbon.

Pirate's treasure party

The thought of hidden treasure is enough to excite anyone, and kids will have a blast at this party. Have each child decorate a treasure chest (for example, a shoebox) and label it with his or her name. In advance, you will have to scout out hiding places (as many as you have guests) and draw a treasure map for each child. When the treasure chests are ready, secretly fill each one with plastic jewels, fake coins, and maybe even slip in a real silver dollar. Then hide each box in its own hiding place. Give each kid a map and let them all hunt. You may want an extra adult or teenager to help if your pirates are small. This party is so action-packed that you won't need games or additional prizes.

Invitation ideas
♦ Message in a bottle.
♦ Construction paper cut or folded into a pirate's hat.

Menu
♦ Cake and ice cream.
♦ Lemonade or milk.

Party favors
♦ Cardboard swords.
♦ Eye patches (party stores have them).
♦ Bandannas.
♦ Pirate hats (folded newspaper or black construction paper).
♦ Their treasure chests filled with treasure.

Beauty parlor party

Most young girls are fascinated with make-up, nail polish, and hair accessories. Enlist several friends to help you with this party and have them bring curling irons, hot rollers, makeup mirrors, and any old cosmetics and nail polish they are willing to donate. Turn your living room into a salon with a hair station, a make-up area, and a station for nails. Ask guests to come dressed in dress-up clothes, hats and high-heels. Perhaps some young boys can come in as customers for a haircut.

Invitation ideas

- An inexpensive comb with a tag attached.
- A compact made from construction paper and aluminum foil.

Menu

- Finger sandwiches.
- Cake and ice cream.
- Pink lemonade.

Party favors

- Trial-sized cosmetics and nail polish.
- Colored hair gel.
- Small hand mirrors.
- Barrettes or hair bows.
- Before and after pictures.

Day at the beach party

If your child has a summer birthday, count your blessings. Backyard parties are fun for kids and easier for you. Any party involving water is a big hit, and when you throw in a couple of wading pools, the sprinkler, water balloons, and maybe a sandbox, you can be sure your guests will be talking about the party for months. Round up several plastic wading pools by borrowing them or buying the inflatable ones for a couple of dollars each. Fill them with water, leaving one for sand if you want it. (Building supply stores sell bags of clean sand.)

Have the following items on hand: balloons, bubble solution and wands, plastic beach buckets, and squirt guns. Tell guests to wear bathing suits and to bring a towel. Recruit at least one other adult to help, and get out of the way.

Invitation ideas

- Beach ball (you can write on it with a permanent marker).
- Sand shovel with a tag attached.

Menu
- Grilled hot dogs.
- Chips.
- Cupcakes—all served outside picnic-style.

Game ideas
- Water balloon toss.
- Buried treasure in the sand (hide tiny plastic toys and pennies in the sand for little kids to find).
- Water gun arcade (set up plastic cups for targets).

Party favors
- Inexpensive plastic shovels and pails.
- Cheap sunglasses.
- Water guns.

Prizes
- Bottles of bubbles.
- Fancy bubble wands.
- Small sand toys.
- Small wind-up water toys.

Sports party

Many children will love the idea of a sports party. This is an outdoor party and the possibilities are endless. Line up some dads and moms to be "officials." Your party can be based on a specific sport (such as a baseball party), or it can be more general. If the kids will be playing a game that requires teams, have an adult divide the group. If the kids have to choose sides, someone's feelings will get hurt.

Invitation ideas
- Pennants made from construction paper or felt. (If using felt, attach a tag with party specifics.)
- Baseballs (or footballs or basketballs) made from construction paper.

Menu

- ◆ Hot dogs.
- ◆ Chips.
- ◆ Bottled root beer.
- ◆ Roasted peanuts in the shell.
- ◆ Cupcakes.

Game ideas

- ◆ Ball toss (use a bucket or a laundry basket for a target).
- ◆ Three-legged race.
- ◆ Kick ball.
- ◆ Long jump.
- ◆ Relay races.

Party favors

- ◆ Baseball caps.
- ◆ Trading cards.
- ◆ Miniature sports balls.

Prizes

- ◆ Olympic-style medals (made from cardboard circles and hung around the child's neck with a ribbon).
- ◆ Blue ribbons (party supply stores have them).

Scavenger hunt

This party is great for pre-teens. Create a list of unusual items, and ask your neighbors if they will participate. If your neighbors are game, you can "plant" certain items in their homes. (Kids don't go into the neighbors' houses. They simply ring the bell and ask the neighbors if they have any item on the list.) Include items that can be found outdoors in the yard, too, such as a brick or leaves from a certain type of tree.

Break the group into teams of three or four, depending on the number of guests. Give each group a list, the parameters of the hunt (such as your street, block, or certain neighbor's houses), and set a time limit. Tell everyone to report back as soon as time is up, whether they've found all the things on the list or not. Because this party is one big game, additional activities are unnecessary. You can award prizes for most items found, least items found, fastest hunt, most unusual item found, and so on.

Invitation ideas
♦ Magnifying glass with a tag attached.
♦ Mini notebook with invitation written on the first page.

Menu
♦ Cake and ice cream.
♦ Soft drinks.

Prizes
♦ Search-and-find puzzle books.
♦ Age-appropriate mystery paperbacks.

The soaring cost of sending kids to school

Once upon a time, public schools were an inexpensive—bordering on free—way to educate your children. (We're not counting taxes, you pay those regardless.) These days public school still may be the most inexpensive route, but it sure isn't cheap.

School supplies gone wild

Remember when "school supplies" meant a couple of pencils, a three-ring binder, a pack of loose-leaf notebook paper, some crayons, and a cigar box to hold them? Not anymore. Now you may have to buy many of the following items: paper towels, tissues, toilet paper, rulers, zipper-style storage bags, glue (three kinds), dry-erase pens for the teacher to use, large boxes of crayons, scissors, reams of printer paper (white and colored), a dozen folders in specified colors, more pencils than one child could possibly use, markers, large packs of construction paper, liquid soap, thousands of sheets of notebook paper, and a calculator. And that's just the basic list. Individual teachers may have additional requirements. No matter where you buy it, you're looking at about $50 worth of stuff per child. As if that weren't enough, you can expect a mid-year note directing you to replenish depleted supplies.

We wish we had an answer to the outrageous school supply situation, but we don't. You may be tempted to simply refuse to send everything the school wants, but this just backfires. Teachers (who shall remain nameless) have told us the supply list is so ridiculous partly because some parents don't provide their children with even the most basic supplies, like paper and pencils. In effect, schools are already forcing conscientious parents to unwittingly fund a school supply welfare program. So, the parent who tries to make a statement by not meeting all of the school's supply demands only succeeds in making a bad situation worse. (However, if you can instigate a school-wide revolt, you might make a lasting impression.)

The best suggestion we can offer is to watch for sales and stock up throughout the year. Keep the supply list as a guide. At least this way you can spread the cost over the entire year, rather than taking a big hit every September.

School fund raisers

Anyone who doesn't know that public schools can't manage to make ends meet with existing funds must have spent the last decade living on Mars. Schools everywhere have turned to fund raising to make up the difference. Fund raising comes in several forms: corporate sponsorship, events like festivals or dinners, and sales drives of various kinds. We don't have a problem with corporate sponsorship (except that it tends to increase in-school advertising), and school events are usually fun.

It's the sales that sometimes literally drive us up the wall. Bake sales are fine because all merchandise is donated and all proceeds go directly to the school, but sales based on glossy brochures full of candy, wrapping paper, or knickknacks are a different story. You should know that the school receives only a small portion of the money generated by these sales, so if you spend $10 on wrapping paper, the school only gets a couple of dollars. If you do want to contribute financially you're better off ignoring the fund raiser and writing a check directly to the school. That way the school gets your entire contribution, you don't accumulate heaps of expensive junk, and you can claim it as a charitable donation at tax time.

Teacher gifts

As long as we're on the subject of school, have you ever wondered what teachers do with the 18 coffee mugs and 12 personalized paperweights they receive from students? And did you know that public school teachers typically spend hundreds of dollars of their own money on classroom equipment each year? If your child gives his or her teacher a present at holiday time, try giving a gift certificate to the teacher's supply store for a change. You could even pool funds with other parents in the class and give a substantial amount. The teacher receives something practical, and you get more value for your dollar by giving a present that will be appreciated. That's what gift giving is all about, anyway.

Chapter 10

Good Housekeeping on a Shoestring

If you look up the word "efficient" in the dictionary, you will find definitions like "productive of desired effects" or "production without waste." We see efficiency as the union of perfectionism and laziness, and this describes our housekeeping philosophy perfectly. We want our households to run smoothly, look presentable, and be comfortable, with as little sustained effort on our part as possible. We want pleasant, even gracious, surroundings without going over budget. We also want to keep our homes in the best possible condition because, having scaled down our lifestyle and material expectations, we aren't going to be trading up anytime soon.

Keeping utility bills in line

Frugality has many benefits, and our favorite perk is that saving money in one area leaves you with more money to spend in another. Like grocery bills, utility costs can be reduced immediately by doing nothing more than applying a little forethought and self-discipline. If you're willing to invest some extra time and money, you can probably save even more. We've all heard of overzealous cost-cutters who refuse to turn on the heat all winter, forcing their families to sleep in overcoats, or limit everyone's hot showers to 90 seconds. If we took this approach, maybe we *could* get our power bills under $30 a month, but who wants to live like that?

We may be frugal, but we're not masochists. On the other hand, why pay more for something when you can spend less and never notice the difference? We've found easy ways to shave off a little here and there off utility bills without sacrificing comfort. If you haven't already contacted your local utility company for information on saving energy, do it now. Remember to ask whether your utility provider offers energy audits to customers. Even if they charge a fee for the audit, it should pay for itself quickly in the form of lower utility bills.

Heating and air conditioning

Keeping your home a comfortable temperature year-round is your single biggest energy expense. If you don't let this cost you any more than it has to, everyone will be more comfortable in the long run.

♦ Clean or replace your air filters every month.

♦ Adjust your thermostat down in the winter and up in the summer. If you dress appropriately, you won't notice a few degrees difference anywhere except on your power bill.

♦ Have your heating and air-conditioning unit(s) serviced regularly.

♦ Take advantage of temperate weather and open windows. This saves energy usage and improves indoor air quality.

♦ Close the vents and shut the door to rooms no one "lives" in like guestrooms, the utility room, and the downstairs bathroom.

♦ Use fans instead of air conditioning whenever practical.

Projects for long-term savings

♦ Install ceiling fans if you don't already have them. Ceiling fans have come down considerably in price, and will keep you comfortable even if your thermostat is set at an energy-saving temperature. Run your ceiling fans on high in the summer to cool a room and on low in the winter to push heat down from the ceiling.

♦ Install extra insulation in your attic. Many older houses are not adequately insulated, and many newer houses could benefit from additional insulation. A comprehensive home-owner's manual will have instructions on doing it yourself.

♦ Stop air leaks. There's no need to heat and cool the great outdoors. Here's how to find leaks. On a windy day, close all doors and windows and light a candle. Hold the flame in front of every door and window. If the flame flickers, you've found a leak. Install weather-stripping and check to make sure your caulk is holding. Caulk is applied to the exterior of your home wherever two different materials meet, such as the area where a brick wall abuts a wooden window casing. If the bottom edges of doors are the culprits, check into installing thresholds or sweeps.

♦ Plant trees and shrubs around your house. Deciduous trees will shade your house in the summer, but allow warming sunlight to hit your home in the winter. Shrubs planted close to your house act as additional insulation. This isn't a quick fix, but you can speed up the process by planting fast-growing trees and shrubbery. Ask your local nursery about landscape plants that grow quickly in your area.

Water usage and your water heater

Because your water heater is probably your second-largest energy user, it makes sense to keep it operating efficiently and to conserve hot water. While you're at it, conserve your unheated water, too.

♦ Make sure your water heater is adequately insulated.

♦ Fix drippy faucets promptly.

♦ Insulate your hot water pipes.

♦ Install water-saving showerheads in the showers and aerators on faucets.

♦ Put a timer on your water heater. Unless your family keeps very irregular hours, there's not much point in having on-demand hot water at 2 a.m. Set your water heater to go off at bedtime and to come back on a half-hour before you get up.

♦ Turn off your water heater when you go out of town.

♦ Put a couple of bricks in your toilet tank. Your toilet will flush just the same, yet use less water.

♦ Use the sprinkler after sundown. The water won't evaporate as quickly and you won't have to water so often. Only water plants and shrubs when needed and don't worry about the lawn.

♦ Never run a half-full dishwasher.

Note: We are *not* recommending lowering the thermostat on your water heater to 120 degrees. Your hot water should reach 140 degrees to kill many germs and parasites. The old theory was that most dishwashers have heaters that get dishes that hot, regardless of water temperature. The current realization is that dirty dishes aren't the only place nasty microbes are found. Turn your water heater back up and take care that young children don't scald themselves.

The telephone

The quickest way to reduce your phone bill is to reduce your long-distance calling. Beyond that, try the following suggestions:

♦ Shop around for the long-distance plans that best meets your needs. Different companies offer different rates depending on a number of factors, including: whether you're calling in or out of state, how many minutes of long distance you use each month, whether you call from home or away, and what time of day you usually call. Look at the whole plan, not just the advertised rate. Don't hesitate to check out some of the smaller long-distance companies now that call quality has become pretty consistent.

♦ Consider canceling extras such as call waiting, Caller ID, and voice mail. If you pay $6 a month for voice mail, a $30 answering machine will pay for itself in five months.

♦ Pore over your phone bill every month. It's not uncommon to find that you've been charged for mystery calls. It's also not uncommon to find that you've been paying for extra services you didn't know you had.

Washer and dryer

Hail the automatic washing machine and the electric dryer! What would we do without them? For one thing, we'd all have lower utility bills. But who wants to give up these conveniences? Here are a few suggestions:

♦ Strive to wash full loads.

♦ If you have to wash small loads separately, dry them together.

♦ Pre-soak heavily soiled loads so you don't have to do them twice.

♦ Use the correct water temperature.

♦ Clean your lint filter after every load.

♦ Make sure your dryer is vented properly and that the duct is unobstructed.

♦ Dry several loads of clothes, one after the other, while the dryer is still warm.

♦ Hang an outdoor clothesline and use it. If you hate scratchy towels, dry them on the clothesline and fluff them in the dryer for five minutes.

♦ Use an indoor drying rack on the days you don't use the clothesline. You can also put clothes on hangers and hang them on your shower rod in the bathroom.

♦ If your power company has a lower rate for off-peak hours, do the laundry when rates are cheaper whenever possible.

Refrigerators and freezers

These two machines are your kitchen's biggest energy hogs. Keeping your refrigerator and freezer in good shape will cut back on energy waste and extend the life of these expensive appliances.

♦ Keep the coils clean and unobstructed.

♦ Never block the interior air vents.

♦ For maximum food safety, keep your refrigerator at 37 to 40 degrees and set your freezer at zero.

♦ Leave enough room between foods for air to circulate.

♦ Make sure your refrigerator (and upright freezer, if you have one) sits level so the door will seal properly.

♦ Make sure your freezer is full. If you don't have enough food to fill it, add plastic jugs of water or bags of ice.

The stove

For some reason, when cutting back on energy usage most people don't think much about the stove.

♦ In summer, use an outdoor grill as much as possible. You won't be using your stove or oven, and your air conditioner won't have to work so hard.

♦ When cooking indoors, use a toaster oven, microwave, electric skillet, or crockpot whenever you can. All of these appliances use much less energy than the stove.

♦ Match the size of the food to the size of the pot, and match the size of the pot to the size of the burner. You'll use your stove's heat output more efficiently.

♦ Whenever possible, cook several dishes in the oven at once.

♦ In general, oven cooking uses less energy than stovetop cooking. If you have a choice, pick the oven.

♦ When you cook on the stovetop, use lids whenever you can.

Lighting

Following are things you can do beyond switching off lights when you leave the room:

♦ If you usually leave a light on all night, use a couple of 4-watt nightlights instead.

♦ Install dimmers on overhead lights.

♦ Make your wattage work for you. If you don't need particularly bright light, put a lower-wattage bulb in your fixture. If you do need bright light, a single high-wattage bulb may be more effective than two mid-range bulbs. For example, one 100-watt bulb will seem brighter than two 60-watt bulbs and you'll save 20 watts of energy. Don't use more wattage than your fixture recommends, however.

♦ If you need additional brightness, dust your bulbs before you switch to a higher wattage. The difference will be noticeable, and may be enough to do the trick.

Frugal household management

If saving money is a good thing, then saving money while alleviating chaos and increasing your spare time is even better. Remember why you quit work in the first place. Wasn't it to take control of your time and your future, to get more enjoyment out of your life while allowing your family to do the same, and to actually *raise* your children rather than letting them just grow up? We think that running your household efficiently is an integral part of all that. The trick is to conserve both time and money while getting as much of your home on auto-pilot as you can.

The laundry room

Oh, what we wouldn't give to be able to report that we had found a way to eradicate laundry and still stay on budget! Alas, we can't; and we're far from alone. According to Procter & Gamble, Americans wash 35 billion loads of laundry per year. That's 100 million tons of laundry! But you can make it easier on yourself by having a system.

We've found that doing laundry once a week makes for one excruciating laundry day, so we suggest you plan to do laundry at least two days each week. At least this way, you can probably confine laundry to a morning or afternoon that you're planning to be home anyway. Here are some other ideas for taking the sting out of doing laundry.

♦ Install a shelf in your laundry area to organize detergent, softener, bleach, and stain removers.

♦ Turn jeans and dark-colored cottons inside out before washing. They won't fade as quickly.

♦ Close zippers and other fasteners to keep them from snagging things.

♦ Fold clothes as soon as they're finished drying to cut down on ironing. This also cuts down on your having to fold piles of laundry the size of Mount Fuji.

♦ Keep a clean bucket in your laundry room for pre-soaking stained clothing. We keep the bucket filled with pre-soak solution (¼ cup powdered detergent, ½ cup borax, a gallon or more cold water) and toss stained clothes into the bucket to soak until laundry day rolls around again. Make sure that there is enough solution in the bucket to completely cover the clothes so they don't mildew in warm weather. (Please be *extremely* careful with buckets if you have babies and toddlers. A small child can drown in a bucket of liquid. If you have little ones and want to use the bucket method, use a bucket with a tight-fitting lid and keep it well above floor level.)

♦ Use bleach only when needed. Although nothing beats bleach for whitening power, it will break down the fibers in your clothes.

♦ Stock up on cheap, plastic laundry baskets from the dollar store. Use several in your laundry room to pre-sort clothes. Put one in every bedroom closet and also in the bathroom if one will fit. A good chore for children is to have them haul up their own filled basket to the laundry room, separating their white clothes in the whites basket, towels in the towel basket, and so on.

♦ Taking good care of the clothing you have ultimately means buying fewer clothes. Follow care instructions, drip-dry cottons whenever possible, and sort clothes ruthlessly to avoid bleeding. If an article of clothing needs mending, do the mending before you wash it.

♦ Even if you have a lot of sewing equipment, keep a small kit with needles, several basic colors of thread, a seam ripper, a pincushion, and sharp scissors in a handy place. If these items are convenient, you're more likely to do minor mending before it turns into major mending.

♦ If something is in great shape but is faded enough to look ratty, use fabric dye to restore the color. Dyes work best with natural fibers. This is also a great trick for black separates. Black clothes from different dye lots rarely match, but they will match if you put them in a black dye bath together.

- Have everyone over 5 put away his own clothes. If you can teach a 3-year-old to do it, more power to you!
- If you've worn something for only a few hours, hang it back up rather than tossing it in the hamper.

The kitchen

A smarter kitchen makes cooking easier and makes cleaning faster and more effective.

- When you're cooking, keep your sink full of hot, soapy water. Training yourself to wash up as you go will make after-meal clean-ups much quicker, and you'll use the dishwasher less.
- A 50-50 solution of vinegar and water will clean your stovetop. Keep it in a spray bottle. You can also use it to spot-clean the kitchen floor between moppings.
- Once a month put an open glass container of ammonia in your oven and leave it overnight. In the morning, the ammonia fumes will have loosened baked-on gunk enough for you to wipe it off. You'll never need expensive oven cleaners or hour-long scrubbing sessions again.
- Consider hanging your pots and pans on an overhead rack for easy access and more room in your cabinets.
- A shelf installed around the perimeter of the room near the ceiling is a good place for little-used kitchen equipment and large serving pieces.
- To clean the microwave: Fill a glass container with ½ cup vinegar and ½ cup water and cook it on high for five minutes. The nuked-on crud will wipe right off. Pouring the used vinegar solution down the drain will help keep the drain clear.
- A hanging wire-mesh basket is good for holding fruits and vegetables that don't require refrigeration, and keeps them off your countertop.
- Keep the utensils that you use daily in a pitcher or utensil holder near the stove.

♦ Many (if not most) cases of the "stomach flu" are actually food-borne illnesses. Wash dishes, cutting boards, and utensils well, and don't be cavalier about kitchen cleanliness. A 10-percent bleach solution (one part bleach to nine parts water) will disinfect countertops, faucet handles, stove handles and controls, the refrigerator handle, and cabinet and drawer pulls. Keep it in a spray bottle and use it often. (Test it in an inconspicuous area first.) Pour a little of the solution in a saucer and soak your kitchen sponge, and replace sponges frequently.

Also, change your dishtowel at least once a day. We've found a great source for inexpensive dishtowels. Large building supply stores sell small towels for use as painting rags. The ones we've seen are regular white terry towels with hemmed edges. They're usually sold by the dozen for a few dollars. As far as we can tell, they're no different from any other white terry dishtowels except that they're about *one-fifteenth* the price. Because they're cheap and white, you can disinfect them regularly with hot water and bleach.

♦ Make room in a lower cupboard for unbreakable dishes and cups so your kids can reach them. Let your kids know what they can have as snacks, and store those at kid-level, too.

♦ Keep a supply of rags in the kitchen. Get in the habit of using a rag whenever possible to cut down on buying paper towels. Toss the rags in laundry after you use them.

The bathroom

Nobody likes to clean the bathroom, but it's quick and easy if you never let it get too bad in the first place.

♦ Clean the bathroom frequently. Keep a 50-50 vinegar and water solution in a spray bottle in the bathroom. Every two or three days take a minute to wipe down surfaces. Once a week, scrub the tub with baking soda (use as you would scouring powder) and clean the toilet by putting ½ cup of baking soda in the bowl and adding a cup of vinegar. When the fizzing stops, clean the inside of the bowl with a toilet brush.

♦ Make chrome fixtures shine by wiping them with rubbing alcohol.

♦ To retard the growth of mold and mildew, dry the inside of the shower after use. You can use a regular towel or a squeegee.

♦ If you do get mold and mildew, you should know that cheap household bleach works just as well as commercial mildew removers.

♦ Baking soda added to bath water will soften and soothe skin and cut down on scummy tub rings.

♦ If you display decorative towels on your bathroom towel bars, hang an over-the-door towel bar on the back of the bathroom door for bath and hand towels.

♦ If your linen closet is tiny or nonexistent, use baskets to hold extra towels and washcloths.

♦ A hanging three-tiered wire mesh basket (the kind used in the kitchen for vegetables) is a fantastic place to stow bathroom clutter such as tub toys, fancy bath products, extra soap, combs and brushes, or even rolled washcloths or hand towels. You can hang the baskets from the ceiling or the shower rod.

♦ Plastic freezer containers are terrific for holding makeup, hair do-dads, medicines, etc. They also stack easily in your bathroom cabinets.

♦ If your bathroom has no storage space, install shelves. If you have a pedestal sink, put a skirt on it and use the hidden floor space underneath for storage.

Kids' bedrooms

You'll do less yelling if your kids can keep rooms tidy themselves.

♦ Use colorful milk crates to store toys, games, and books. They're stackable and can also be used as closet cubbyholes to hold shoes or stacks of folded clothes.

♦ Install a shelf at your child's eye level that runs all the way around the room to hold stuffed animals, trophies, and books.

♦ Kids are natural packrats, so help them keep knickknacks, papers, and doo-dads at a minimum. Tell your kids that any broken toys or half-complete puzzles and games are going in the garbage. You'll be able to clear out some useless junk, and after a couple of trips to the dump, your kids will start taking great care of their things. Let their packrat tendencies work to your advantage and, ultimately, theirs!

♦ Put up a large corkboard to show off artwork or school papers.

♦ Hang an extra clothes bar halfway between the regular clothes bar and the closet floor. This allows kids to hang up their own clothes and doubles the closet space. Use the higher bar to hang out-of-season things.

♦ Used stackable plastic containers with lids to store crayons, game pieces, and collections of tiny things.

♦ Have your child vacuum the floor from time to time with a hand-held vacuum.

♦ Keep stuffed animals clean. Put machine-washable toys in a pillowcase, tie the pillowcase, and toss it in the washer and then the dryer. Sprinkle unwashable animals with baking soda and allow to sit for several hours. Shake and then brush off the baking soda.

♦ Enforce the eternal Rule of Toys: When you're done playing with something, you must put it away before you get out anything else.

Your bedroom

You should make your bedroom an attractive, enticing, and relaxing place, and keeping it organized and clutter-free is good way to start. Create a private retreat and fill it with things you love.

♦ Attach hangers or hooks to the inside of your closet door to hold scarves, belts, and ties.

♦ If you're short on drawer space, use decorative boxes to hold pantyhose and other lingerie.

- Keep out-of-season clothes in boxes in the top of the closet or under the bed.
- Use an over-the-door shoe holder in your closet.
- Stash furniture polish and a dusting cloth in your closet. This makes it easier to stay on top of dusting.
- Get a handle on stacks of paperback books by storing them in your closet on an over-the-door wire rack.
- An old cedar chest or steamer trunk makes an attractive storage place for quilts, bed linens, or out-of-season clothes.
- Go through closets and drawers and box up anything that you or your partner no longer wear. Seal the box, put it in the garage, and leave it for a year. If you never have to dig anything out of the box during the year it lives in the garage, it's safe to get rid of the clothes permanently. Take them to a consignment shop to sell, share with friends, or give them to charity.
- Invest in some scented candles. They won't help you keep your room clean or save you any money, but your room will smell wonderful and everyone looks better by candlelight.

The living room or den

The room where your family spends the most time is the room you spend the most effort keeping neat.

- Try to cut down on clutter by keeping knickknacks to a bare minimum. If you must have knickknacks, consider putting a shelf 18 inches from the ceiling all the way around the room. You'll be able to see your treasures, but you'll never have to straighten them, and you'll hardly ever have to dust them.
- Don't let stacks of newspapers and magazines get knee-deep. If you need to keep a magazine for some reason, clip out the part you want and throw the rest in the recycling bin.
- If you have a baby or a toddler, keep a pretty wicker basket in the living room to hold toys.

♦ Use pretty boxes to hold items such as magazines, videos, or craft projects in progress. Hatboxes work well and can be purchased inexpensively at craft stores. Stacked three high, hatboxes can also double as a small side table.

♦ Look for dual-purpose furniture. An old trunk makes a sturdy, casual coffee table and can hold extra bedding or games. A small filing cabinet draped with yards of beautiful fabric is the perfect height to hold a large houseplant.

♦ Install an over-the-door rack on the inside of your coat closet to hold your video collection.

♦ Use coasters under drinks. To make inexpensive coasters, buy ceramic tiles (often less than a dollar each, even for hand-painted ones) and glue felt to back.

♦ To clean miniblinds, close the blinds and vacuum them using the dusting attachment on your vacuum. If your blinds get really grimy, take them down and lay them in the kid's wading pool. Fill the pool with warm soapy water and a little bleach (for white blinds), and soak the blinds for about an hour. Scrub stubborn dirt as needed and rinse. You'll have clean blinds and a sparkling wading pool.

The garage

If you have a garage, you probably use it more for storage than anything else. It's worth it to keep it reasonably well-organized so you can find things when you need them. You'll be surprised how much less hassle yard work is if you can actually find the tools.

♦ Install a pegboard and use it to hang tools in plain view.

♦ Use as much sturdy but inexpensive shelving as you can.

♦ Nail jar lids to the undersides of wooden shelves. Fill jars with nails, screws, tacks, fuses, or anything else tiny enough to get lost. Screw the filled jars into the lids. Little things will be easy to see and easy to get to.

♦ Use large "S" hooks to hang ladders, bikes, and sleds from the rafters.

♦ Plastic milk crates make good, portable storage containers for sporting equipment, craft supplies, and more.

The home finance center

Whether you have a full-fledged home office or a paper bag to hold the bills, having your household finances organized is a must.

◆ Schedule time each month to pay your bills. Because different bills tend to come due on different days, you might want to schedule two days to pay bills, for example, the 1st and the 15th of each month.

◆ Find a place, like a drawer or a basket, to hold bills that are waiting to be paid. When a bill arrives, put it directly into the bill holder. This way, no bills are ever misplaced or forgotten.

◆ Keep all of your bill-paying supplies in one spot, preferably with the bills. You'll need a pen, a calculator, envelopes, and stamps.

◆ If the due dates of your bills are spread out and you'd like to have them better aligned with your paychecks, call creditors and ask if they will adjust your billing cycle. Many creditors will simply ask you what due date you'd prefer.

◆ Don't pay your bills late. Late fees are never frugal.

◆ Remember that your bank charges you for its services and you should make sure you're getting a good deal. Most banks have several checking account options, all with a different monthly fee. The differences are usually tied to age, minimum balance, number of checks written per month, overdraft services, debit card or ATM usage, and whether you have additional accounts at the same bank. Periodically review your bank's various checking accounts. Is your current account still your best option? Also, check out the competition from time to time.

◆ You can't pay any more for checks than you do buying them through your banker. Although ordering replacement checks through your bank is far and away the most convenient option, you're paying triple for the service. Look into mail-order checks. There are several very reputable companies around.

The case for all-white linens

If you're serious about simplifying the upkeep of your household, consider converting to all-white linens. They're so much easier. Here's why:

♦ Once upon a time your towels may have all matched. Now you may have a hodgepodge collection of various colors. Remember the year you bought towels in aubergine? That was the only year they made them in that color! Part of the beauty of having nothing but white towels is that new white towels will match old white towels and middle-aged white towels. A stack of clean white towels will give your bathroom the "spa look." And the manufacturers always make white!

♦ The same thing goes for your sheets. How many orphan flat sheets do you have in your linen closet? If all your sheets are white and the elastic on your fitted sheet wears out, just buy another white fitted sheet and, *voila*!, your set is complete again.

♦ It's easy to find white linens on sale or in discount or outlet stores.

♦ Any store that carries linens will carry a good selection of white linens.

♦ White never fades.

♦ White linens look cleaner.

♦ White linens are cleaner. Brightly colored sheets and towels have to be washed in cold water, whereas even 100-percent white cotton sheets and towels can be washed in hot. One of the most common allergens and a leading trigger of asthma is dust mites. To kill them, experts say linens must be laundered in water that is 130 degrees or more. Some experts even argue that cold-water washing of bedding may partially account for the sharp rise in allergies, the ear infections that accompany them, and asthma over the past two decades.

♦ If you have to, you can always bleach white linens.

Rethinking household cleaners

Keeping your home clean can keep you in the red if you buy dozens of specialty cleaning products at $3 a pop. The following recipes call for ingredients you already have. Not only are these homemade cleaners much cheaper, but you don't have to deal with so many bottles and cans under your kitchen sink. Of course, you should never, ever, mix ammonia and bleach, as the combination produces toxic fumes, and you should always test any cleaner first.

All-purpose glass cleaner

One part white vinegar.
One part water.
Mix in a spray bottle.

This leaves glass and other hard surfaces just as clean as a commercial glass cleaner. Vinegar is a mild disinfectant and has anti-fungal properties. If athlete's foot is a problem, use vinegar full strength to wipe down the bottom of the shower stall and bathroom floor, too. As a bonus, it's non-toxic. Once cured, your athlete can even dab vinegar on his feet to prevent the fungus from coming back.

Mildew remover and general disinfectant

One part bleach
Nine parts water
Mix in a spray bottle

Use in kitchen and bathroom as needed. Never mix with ammonia.

Mild abrasive scrub

Use baking soda in place of scouring powder. Baking soda has whitening power on its own, but if more whitening action is needed, you can make a paste of baking soda and a little bleach. Wear rubber gloves.

Floor cleaner

Check the manufacturer's recommendations for your particular flooring, but you should be able to use either one-half cup of ammonia in a gallon of water or a cup of vinegar in a gallon of water for mopping.

Drain cleaner

¼ cup baking soda
½ cup vinegar

Pour baking soda down the drain and follow with the vinegar. Close the drain until the fizzing stops, then flush with boiling water. To keep drains clear, do this once a month.

Homemade dryer sheets

Small sponge or large sponge cut in thirds
One part bottled fabric softener
Three parts water

Combine fabric softener and water in a small container with a lid. Dip the sponge in solution and throw in the dryer, just as you would a dryer sheet.

You can use the same sponge over and over without having to wash it. A bottle of fabric softener is the same price or less than expensive commercial dryer sheets and, used this way, will last a year or more.

Copper cleaner

If your copper is lightly tarnished, you can clean it with ketchup or hot pepper sauce. Just spread on the surface, let sit for a few minutes and rinse well. If the copper is more heavily tarnished, clean it with three parts flour, one part salt, and enough ammonia to make a paste.

Gold jewelry cleaner

You can clean jewelry with toothpaste and an old, soft-bristled toothbrush. Always be careful cleaning stones, you can loosen the settings.

When you need new stuff

No matter how carefully you shop, or how well you take care of the possessions you already have, there will be times when you have to buy or replace an appliance or a piece of furniture. The bigger the ticket price, the more prices fluctuate, so it always pays to shop around. But before you ever begin to shop for durable goods, decide what you really need and want, and consider buying used.

We've known many people who turn up their noses at the thought of buying second-hand merchandise, but these people seem to equate "used" with "second-rate" or "shabby." On the other hand, we know people who seek out used durable goods whenever possible. When this group hears "used" they think, "less expensive," or "potentially higher quality at an affordable price." Guess which group tends to buy more high-quality goods without spending a fortune? People who are serious about saving money know that the key to finding just what you want (whether new or used) at a good price is to anticipate your needs and start looking before your need becomes urgent.

Of course, the idea of buying used goods isn't totally unfamiliar to any of us. We do it all the time with houses, cars, and antiques. Why not do it with other things, too? Next time you're in the market for a big-ticket item like a sofa or a refrigerator, by all means look at what's available new, but remember to consider what may be available second-hand. You're bound to expand your range of choices, if nothing else.

Thrift stores

People who have the best luck at thrift stores have learned to look for *potential* rather than perfection. Although "potential" may not be what you're looking for in a major appliance, it may be exactly what you want in furniture.

If you've ever tried to shop for a new sofa, you probably know the routine. You look at your living room furniture, gather up fabric swatches and paint chips, and head to the furniture stores. At the end of the day, you've been to 15 stores. Eleven were having going-out-of-business sales and the other four were offering "everything must go!" close-out prices. All the stores were selling sofas so ugly that it's a wonder they weren't paying customers to haul them off. The average price for an ugly sofa was $1,500. Finally you make your way to the custom furniture store, where you can choose your own style and up-holstery. The styles are classic, the furniture is well-made, and the fabrics are gorgeous. You find exactly what you want, but it costs $4,000. To buy it you'd need a second mortgage.

If you're smart, your next stop is the thrift store. Maybe you have to check back several times over the next few weeks. Finally, they have what you're looking for: an older sofa with classic lines. It's covered in an ugly brown and avocado plaid material, circa 1967. They're asking $75 dollars for it. You buy it, and have slipcovers made for about $600, including the price of nice fabric. For about $700, you have the sofa you wanted in the first place, at less than half the price.

Thrifts stores are also a good place to find small appliances. You'll see everything from waffle irons to food processors. Most stores have electrical outlets available for testing appliances, and many offer a 30-day warranty, so it's worth a look. Large appliances are not as common, but if you're looking for a chest freezer or a second refrigerator to keep in the garage, you may find one.

The classifieds

Whatever you're shopping for, take time to glance through the classified section of your local paper. When you spot something that sounds good, call immediately because the best buys go in a hurry. While you've got the seller on the phone, ask why they're selling, if the item is still under warranty, or—in the case of appliances—if they will extend a 30-day warranty of their own. Often they'll tell you that there's nothing wrong with whatever it is, but that they've simply decided to change color schemes and it doesn't match anymore. When you're buying from an individual, remember that they've priced the item with room to negotiate.

The classifieds are also the place to find estate sales. Usually these sales include the entire contents of a home, so items offered will run the gamut from linens to fine furniture to kitchenware to tools.

Yard sales

On Fridays, remember to check the paper for yard sales. If someone is selling furniture or appliances, they will almost certainly mention it in the ad. Yard sales will offer the very best prices on most used items, but the quality and availability are spotty. If you're going to a yard sale to find something specific—especially if the item was listed in the ad—get there early.

Scratch-and-dent stores

What happens to the appliances and furniture that are damaged in the warehouse or during shipping? They go to scratch-and-dent stores. Most metropolitan areas have them, but you may have to ask around to find them. You'll find a wonderful selection of brand-new merchandise at up to 50 percent off the retail price due to (often minor) exterior damage.

Mary recently made out like a bandit at her local scratch-and-dent store. She and her husband needed to replace their refrigerator and went shopping at the regular appliance store. The refrigerator they wanted was so far out of their price range that they couldn't even consider it. Ever resourceful, Mary asked the salesperson where the store sent its damaged goods, and he gave her the address to the scratch-and-dent place. There she found a famous brand refrigerator with all the features they wanted for less than what a basic model cost at the appliance store. Because it was brand-new, it carried the regular manufacturer's warranty. The refrigerator had an ugly scratch down one side, which is completely hidden by Mary's kitchen cabinets.

Checklist for a smart shopper

Before you buy:

♦ Carefully consider what you need and what features are important to you.

♦ Compare brands. Ask for recommendations from friends and check magazines and other publications that contain product comparisons.

♦ Plan ahead to take advantage of sales.

♦ Check with the Better Business Bureau to find out if the company is reputable.

♦ Check for extra charges, such as fees for delivery, installation costs, and service costs.

♦ Read warranties carefully.

♦ Read all contracts carefully. Make sure that all blank spaces are filled in before signing.

♦ Make sure you understand the store's return policy before you buy.

♦ Don't assume an item is a bargain just because it is advertised as one.

After you buy:

♦ Read the instructions on how to use the product.

♦ Read and understand the warranty. Check with your state or local consumer office to see if you have any additional warranty rights.

♦ Keep all sales receipts, warranties, and instructions.

♦ If trouble occurs, report it to the company immediately. Don't try to fix it yourself; you run the risk of voiding your warranty.

♦ Keep a file of your efforts to resolve your problems. It should include the name of the person you spoke with, dates of your conversation and the outcome of the conversation. Keep all copies of letters you write to a company.

—U.S. Office of Consumer Affairs

Bartering

Bartering is the time-honored tradition of trading goods and services. Many businesses still do it, and trading is a way of life at flea markets. ("Hey buddy, I'll give you 200 eight-track tapes for that lava lamp you've got there!") Bartering won't work everywhere, but keep it in mind. You may find yourself baby-sitting for your hair-dresser, or doing yard work in exchange for sewing. One caveat: the IRS considers the goods or services you receive via bartering as income, so check with your accountant. Some areas have bartering clubs where members get together to trade services. These clubs will help you keep track of any tax liability you incur.

Become a do-it-yourselfer

Keeping your home in good shape will save you money in the long run, and anything you can do yourself will save you even more. If you're not very handy, you can still learn to do the basics. A good place to start is your local library. Check out several comprehensive books on home maintenance, and when you find one you like, go buy it. A $35 home maintenance manual will pay for itself the first time you don't have to pay an hour's worth of labor to someone who does a 15-minute repair in your home. Also, check with building supply stores, especially the large chains. Many offer inexpensive seminars on a variety of home maintenance or home improvement topics. Even if you don't attend a seminar, staff members are usually very knowledgeable and willing to answer questions or offer advice.

Basic tools every do-it-yourselfer needs

Screwdrivers (include at least a Phillips head and a flathead)
Adjustable wrench
Crowbar
Claw hammer
Pliers (include at least one pair of needle-nose pliers for those tiny jobs, and one pair of wire cutters)
Plane (invaluable when you have to fix a door)
Handsaw
Measuring tape (spring for the good one)
Ice pick (great for punching holes)
Files (gather an assortment of different sizes and types)
Spackle and spatula (comes in handy when you need to fix a dent or hole in the wall)
Nails, screws, nuts, and bolts
Sandpaper (in several grades, from coarse to fine)

Everyone needs to learn at least some basic home maintenance, but there are still some jobs best left to professionals, such as:

- Electrical wiring.
- Working on the heating or air conditioning unit.
- Leaks in the roofing or in the structure of your home.

Remember, if you own a home, your house is the most expensive purchase you will ever make. Doesn't it make sense to protect your investment?

Chapter 11

Vacations, Outings, and Other Fun Stuff

Just because you're living on a budget and watching your spending doesn't mean you have to get yourself and your family stuck in a rut. Everybody needs a break from the daily grind, and families with children may need breaks more than most. Work vacations and other outings into your budget. Remember, you don't have to spend a lot of money to have a lot of fun.

But we always spend a fortune on vacation!

Maybe you can't afford to spend a week living off room service at the Plaza Hotel or visiting every port in the Caribbean, but you can still take a vacation. Vacations can entail almost anything, from a long-awaited (and saved-for) getaway to Disney World to a three-day camping trip. You'll just have to do some research, save some money, set a budget, and stick to it.

First, you will need to decide where you want to go and how long you want to stay. Then take the time to find out how much you can expect to spend. Remember to include the following expenses into your cost estimate:

- ◆ **Cost of travel.** If you're driving, remember to add on-the-road meals to your total cost of travel.
- ◆ **Cost of lodging.** Make sure to check rates and include tips for housekeeping, valets, and other often overlooked incidentals.

157

- **Cost of food.** Figure on at least $10 per person per meal—more if you want to eat in upscale restaurants.
- **Taxes.** Call the chamber of commerce in the area you plan to visit to inquire about tax rates. Many tourist towns have high sales tax and a separate lodging tax.
- **Entertainment and activity costs.** Budget for amusement parks, museums, theme parks, sports activities, and other leisure costs.
- **Cost of souvenirs.** Set a budget for each family member.
- **Miscellaneous spending money.** Plan to have an extra $20 per day for soft drinks, unanticipated admissions, and whatever may come up unexpectedly.

Once you have all your figures for lodging, travel, and tickets to attractions, call a travel agent to see if there are any special rates or discounts available. If the estimated cost is more than you want to spend, you may be able to reduce costs by tinkering with your plans. Here are some ideas:

- You may be able to save significantly by rescheduling your vacation. There are spectacular deals to be found when traveling during the off-season.
- Consider staying in a condo instead of a hotel room. The rates are often comparable, and you will be able to cook rather than eat every meal in a restaurant. To cut back on food costs while still eating out at least some of the time, go to restaurants for less expensive meals such as breakfast or brunch, and have dinner in.
- If you're planning to vacation in a resort area where the lodging is outrageous, start calling hotels located outside the immediate tourist trap. You may find that it's worth it to drive 30 minutes to get the attractions if you can cut your lodging costs in half.
- Rather than jamming in everything you possibly can while you're on vacation, pick one or two attractions and forego the rest.
- Consider taking a three- or four-day vacation instead of a full week.

Disney on a budget

Many kids we know (and some adults) are dying to go to Disney World. Yes, it's expensive, but it doesn't have to be outrageous. Mary and her husband took their children to Disney World recently. They started planning the trip two years in advance, did plenty of research, and managed to fit it in as an extra vacation. They bought tickets to the park in advance, found a condo with a low, off-season rate, and worked hard to keep travel expenses at a minimum. In order to make the most of the time they had, they traveled in January when the crowds are thinner. Mary cooked most of their meals at the condo, and they ate lunch every day in the park. They stayed five days, had a fantastic time, and spent less than $400 dollars on food, souvenirs, and incidentals. Here's Mary's advice for planning:

♦ Start planning a year to 18 months in advance.

♦ Check on discount tickets. Many employers, clubs, and organizations all over the country offer discount tickets. Ask around.

♦ Disney is always crowded, but some weeks tend to be slower than most. Call the park and ask about the slowest times.

♦ Choose a slow week during the off-season, especially early January or just after Labor Day. You'll get the best rates on travel and accommodations.

♦ Estimate a budget based on your research and call a travel agent. Tell the agency your budget requirements and see if it can offer you a better deal.

♦ Make reservations as far in advance as possible.

♦ Get your hands on one of the many Disney travel guides. There are several very good ones in bookstores, and some rate all the attractions and eateries in the various parks.

♦ Getting autographs from Mickey Mouse and the gang is a very big deal for the little ones. Buy an autograph book for each child before your leave home, because the ones sold inside the park are expensive. Remember to bring a pen.

♦ Set a souvenir budget for each child. Make sure children understand they won't be able to buy everything they see, and should consider which souvenirs they want most.

♦ Plan your daily schedule before you leave home. There's absolutely no way to see everything, so know which parks you want to visit and which day you want to visit them.

Once you arrive in Orlando, you will find an onslaught of tourist attractions. You'll be overwhelmed at the sheer numbers of things to do and spend money on. Stick to your plan. Here are Mary's tips for your stay:

♦ Always carry your camera and plenty of film.
♦ Take your travel guide with you to the park—you'll need it.
♦ Visit the attractions you must see first, and visit others as time permits.
♦ Do try to see at least one parade, and arrive early for the best view.
♦ Decide where you want to eat and plan your route accordingly. (The travel guide will be a big help.)
♦ Pace yourself. If your try to cram too much into a day, you'll just get tired feet and cranky kids.
♦ Don't wear new shoes! You will be spending the entire day on your feet, either standing in line or walking miles and miles between attractions. If you have blisters by 10 a.m. the first day, the rest of your trip will be miserable.
♦ Rent a stroller inside the park, and get a double stroller if one's available. This will give you enough room to carry a kid and a lot of stuff.
♦ Have fun!

"Vacation" and "resort" are not synonymous

If the price of a trip to a famous vacation destination takes your breath away, think about a vacation that's cheaper from the start. Here are some more ideas.

Camping

It isn't for everyone, but if you love the great outdoors and you aren't afraid of a few mosquitoes, camping can be a terrific way to vacation inexpensively. If you're new to camping, state and national parks are a good place to start. Hundreds of such parks are sprinkled all across North America and many offer amenities such as swimming pools, lakes, hiking trails, and horseback riding, in addition to a campground. If you plan to camp using the pitch-a-tent method, you must have equipment. Because camping gear can be expensive, we suggest you try to borrow equipment at first. This way you can make sure camping is really for you before making any investments.

Many campgrounds offer reasonably priced cabins, too. The cabins are usually very basic and you may still need sleeping bags, and possibly a camp stove. If you love the idea of camping, but shudder at the thought of really roughing it, you can always check into renting an RV. For information on state parks, call the departments of tourism in the state you want to visit. For general information on national parks, or a brochure on a specific national park, write to:

Department of the Interior
National Park Service
Office of Public Inquiries
P.O. Box 37127, Room 1013
Washington DC 20013-7127
(202) 208-4747

Multifamily vacations

We know many families who vacation with other families in order to pool resources. Often, seaside towns, ski towns, or lakeside areas will have rental condos or houses that sleep 12 or more people. If you split a weekly rental with friends or extended family, you can get your lodging costs for a very reasonable price. If you plan to share a vacation, you'll have much more fun if you discuss the logistics of your plan before you go.

♦ Will you all spend all your time together, or will you have days where each family does something on their own?

♦ How will meals be handled? Will you split groceries, purchase groceries separately, or will you take turns cooking meals for the entire group?

♦ If baby-sitting will be needed, how will you handle it?

♦ Do some of you want to sleep late while others want to hit the beach or the slopes early?

Joint vacations can be wonderful, but only if everyone is considerate of everyone else. Don't plan a joint vacation with a family whose habits and expectations are opposite yours.

Painless ways to save money for your vacation

◆ Cut $10 a week from your grocery budget. You'll save $520 in a year.

◆ Open a vacation savings account and put five dollars in it every week. You'll have saved $260 by the end of the year.

◆ Have a yard sale. You'll get rid of things you don't need and raise anywhere from $100 to $500 toward your vacation.

◆ Put aside half of any windfall money for your vacation.

◆ Have the whole family work to lower utility bills by an additional 10 percent. Put the savings in your vacation fund.

◆ Get in the habit of putting your loose change into a vacation jar or piggy bank.

House swapping

If you have a close friend or relative who lives in another area and your vacations can be arranged to coincide, you might be in a position to try house swapping. You use their home for the week while they use yours.

If you decide to give house swapping a try, there are ways to make the transition painless:

◆ Clarify arrival and departure times.

◆ Let neighbors know that someone other than you will be in your home while you're gone.

◆ Don't leave your pet python for your guest to care for, unless you clear it with him or her (the guest, not the python) first.

◆ If you don't want someone to have to hunt through your closets while you're gone, leave extra linens and such out where they will be seen.

◆ Discuss groceries. If you want to stock the refrigerator for your guests, let them know that the food is there for them.

◆ Leave menus out for restaurants that deliver to your area, as well as directions to the grocery store and local shopping districts.

♦ Leave a list or map of local attractions.

♦ Make sure you make your guests aware of your home's quirks. If you have to kick the bottom of the refrigerator door to make it shut properly, you'll need to tell them.

Local vacation spots

If you want to go on vacation, but both time and funds are limited, consider a vacation spot in your own area. Many of us have wonderful destinations nearby that we never visit because they're so close. The great thing about vacationing locally is that you don't have to spend time or money traveling. You may even want to call your local tourist bureau or visitor's bureau for ideas.

Vacation at home

Think about it: You plan a vacation to take a break from hassles and to spend an enjoyable chunk of time with your family. So what do you do? You run a million errands to prepare for the trip, perform all manner of logistical gymnastics so you can go away without your life falling apart, pack up half of everything you own, load yourselves and your fidgety kids in the car, and rush off to an unfamiliar place that's likely to be crowded. If this sounds more like work than fun to you, take a vacation at home instead.

The trick to enjoying a vacation at home is to act like you're on vacation. Before your vacation starts, clean the house, wash all the laundry, and stock the refrigerator. Plan to do some of the things you don't usually have time to do. Spend a day at a nearby tourist attraction. One afternoon take the kids to a matinee and go out to dinner afterward. Pack a lunch and take a day-long bike ride. Devote the entire week to having fun with the family. The possibilities are endless.

Be a day-tripper

Going places shouldn't be relegated to vacations, and day trips are a fun way to break the monotony of your routine. If you look for interesting places within an hour or two of home, you're bound to find several day-trip destinations.

The zoo. We don't know anyone who doesn't enjoy going to the zoo. If you don't have a zoo in your hometown, check your nearest metropolitan area. Most zoos have picnic areas, so you can pack a lunch and spend the day.

State parks. Most people have a state park within a two-hour drive of home. Call your state department of tourism and ask about parks in your area. Many state parks offer hiking trails, lakes for fishing or swimming, historical museums, or beaches. Picnic areas are practically a given, and entrance fees are affordable.

Museum hopping. Check with your chamber of commerce to locate the art, historical, or science museums in your area. Many museums offer reduced rates or free admittance on certain days to encourage attendance. Call your local museums and ask.

Historic landmarks. Even if you're not a history buff, visiting an historic landmark can be a fascinating way to spend a day. Choices range from historically significant homes or estates to battlefields to important public buildings. Ask your tourist bureau for a listing of historic landmarks in your area.

Regional festivals and fairs. Old-fashioned county fairs are a common fall event in many rural areas, but even in larger cities you can find several annual festivals. We've been to shrimp festivals, arts and crafts festivals, music festivals, and even a covered bridge festival. Look for listings in regional publications and in your local papers.

Explore a nearby town. Get off you own beaten path and go check out a nearby town for the day. Once you get 45 minutes outside of the suburbs, small towns tend to be compact and self-sufficient, often with a small museum, local diners, and quirky shops. Next time someone says, "Such-and-such is a neat little town," take note and plan to visit.

Fun things to do anytime

When we really think about it, the times we enjoyed the most as children weren't the trips our parents planned for weeks on end. They were the things we did as family just because they were fun.

Family togetherness

Here are some ideas for keeping your family together. They are taken from the newsletter *The Parenting Pages*. (More information about this and other newsletters is in the appendix.)

♦ Make it a point to have dinner together several nights a week.

♦ Have a family photo night. Have the whole family get involved in sorting photos and putting them into albums.

♦ Start a birthday tradition. Breakfast out alone with one parent, lunch alone with the other, and dinner with everyone at home.

♦ Write a letter to each child on his or her birthday. Focus on the child's contributions and uniqueness. Save the letters in a safe place, so they can be reread throughout the years.

♦ Turn the TV off one night a week. Play a game, take a walk, or sit at the dinner table for hours.

♦ Invite extended family members to your child's sporting events.

♦ Have everyone in the family pitch in to take care of chores. Do not redo their work even if it's not the way you would do it yourself.

♦ Attend church or a place of worship together.

♦ Create a meaningful holiday tradition for Christmas or Hanukah. Take the focus away from gifts and commercialism and bring it back to just being together.

♦ Keep a weeknight or Sunday afternoon just for the family. Plan to spend the time doing a family activity. Ask for input from everyone.

—Cynthia Edmonds
Editor, *The Parenting Pages*

Movie and pizza night. Instead of renting one movie for the kids and another for yourselves, find a movie that the whole family will enjoy. You can even use this opportunity to introduce your kids to one of your childhood favorites. Make homemade pizza (or spring for pizza delivery), pile everyone into the living room, and have a family pizza-and-film festival.

Play a game. Make a giant bowl of popcorn, gather everybody around the kitchen table, and haul out some old-fashioned board games or a deck of cards. If you get tired of playing old maid or Chinese checkers, teach the kids to play hearts, backgammon, or even poker (keep a bag of pennies or buttons for betting).

Go out for ice cream. Forget the ice cream in the freezer. Every so often, load up the kids after dinner and head to the ice cream parlor for dessert.

Local theater. Expose your children to the magic of the stage without breaking the bank. You may have access to both college and community theater productions. Your local high school may even have a theater department. Check the papers for matinees.

Build a campfire. If you don't have a fireplace, you might be able to build a tiny campfire in your backyard or in a hibachi on your patio. Roast marshmallows and hot dogs and eat them off the stick.

Go stargazing. Grab a blanket and a thermos of hot chocolate and go stargazing. You may have to drive out of town to get away from the city lights. For the most impressive shows, watch the newspaper for the dates of meteor showers that will be visible in your area.

Go camping in your backyard. If you have a backyard, find the sleeping bags, pitch a tent, and take the kids camping. If someone gets too scared to sleep, you can always go back in.

Host a casual potluck dinner. Invite another family with children over for a potluck dinner or barbecue. The kids can play while the parents chat. Potlucks are fun and nobody spends much money.

Attend a sporting event. The cost of attending professional or high-profile college sporting events has skyrocketed, but ticket prices at high schools, community colleges, and even minor-league baseball games are still affordable. Carry enough cash for everybody to get a hot dog and a soft drink. Kids usually don't care who's playing. They get caught up in the excitement regardless.

Eat out on kids-eat-free night. Many family restaurants have a night, usually early in the week, when kids under 12 can eat for free. Because these usually aren't expensive places to begin with, such restaurants can make a family dinner out very affordable.

Catch a movie at the drive-in. Drive-ins are making a comeback across the country, and personally, we're thrilled. Pop a ton of popcorn, grab some soft drinks, and make the most of it. Drive-ins are usually much less expensive than traditional cinemas. Plus, you can talk back to the characters on the screen without disturbing other movie-goers. (Except the ones in your car, of course!)

Take a walk. When the weather is nice, take the entire family out for an old-fashioned stroll around your neighborhood or a nearby park. The exercise is good for everybody, and you'll notice things you usually miss when you whiz by in your car.

Chapter 12

What's In It for *Me?*

The most common complaint we hear from at-home parents is that they never get to do anything for themselves. Heck, that's *our* biggest complaint, too. Being an at-home parent means being on duty 24 hours a day, seven days a week, nonstop. With such a relentless schedule, it's easy to put yourself at the very bottom of your "To-Do" list. But if you don't take a break from time to time, you'll go batty.

Getting out alone or with friends

Every parent at home needs some time away from the family now and then. You may not be bringing home a paycheck, but you're still working hard. Schedule time every week or two when your partner can watch the kids for a couple of hours while you get out of the house. You may not be in a position to perk yourself up by dropping $300 on a new outfit, but there are still plenty of things you can do.

Curl up with a good book. When was the last time you were home alone? Have your spouse take the kids out for an hour or two so you can lounge on the sofa with that novel you've been dying to read.

Attend a lecture. Local colleges or public libraries sometimes offer a lecture series. Call and ask for a schedule.

Go out for coffee. If your budget doesn't accommodate lunches with friends on a regular basis, you can always meet them for coffee.

Craft shows. If you like crafts, watch the newspaper for shows in your area. Even if you don't buy anything, you may come home with some great ideas. Of course, there are also car shows, animal shows (cat, dog, horse—even reptile shows), rock and gem shows, and antique shows, just to name a few.

Get pampered at the beauty school. If you're a working mom who had to break it off with your hairdresser and manicurist when you quit your job, you might enjoy getting the works at your local cosmetology school. The prices are low and instructors are on hand to closely supervise students. Stay-at-home dads can try out these schools for services, as well. If you're leery of students with scissors, you can still get a manicure and have your hair washed and styled.

Just be. Many at-home parents spend so much time doing everything for the family that they never have time to just "be." Consider carving out some time to spend with yourself. You could use this time for thinking, writing, or just observing. You could do this in your home, a church or synagogue, museum, or botanical gardens. You could walk through the woods, or even go people-watching in a park. If you're lucky enough to have them nearby, you could drink in the scenery at the beach or in the mountains. You may find that time alone is so enjoyable that you want to incorporate it into your routine.

The dating game

Remember when you and your spouse were dating? You would go out to dinner, catch a movie, or just enjoy each other's company. You were paying attention to each other all the time. Within a few years, you hardly saw each other alone, ever. What happened?

Real life and small children, that's what.

One of the best things you can do for yourself and your relationship is to start dating again. You might have to set aside a regular time (every Wednesday night or every other Saturday, for example) when the two of you spend a couple of hours alone. The first thing you'll have to do is make arrangements for the kids. Maybe you have a baby-sitting situation that is budget-friendly. If not, you may want to look into working out a trade with another family. For example, you keep their kids every other Tuesday night while they go out, and they keep your children on alternate Tuesdays.

Whenever you need a lift

If you can't get away, but still need a quick pick-me-up, try a few of these homemade spa treatments.

- **Baking soda** is a great (and inexpensive) skin conditioner and polisher. Add ½cup to your bath or use as an occasional facial cleanser.
- **Plain cornmeal** is a terrific facial scrub. It's also cheap enough to use in the shower as a body scrub.
- **Honey** is a soothing treatment for blemished or irritated facial skin. Apply to clean skin and leave on while you soak in a warm bath for 20 minutes.
- **Oatmeal and honey** combined make a moisturizing mask. Use plain uncooked oatmeal and add enough water to make a paste. Add a tablespoon of honey and apply to your face.
- **Beaten egg white** used as a mask will temporarily tighten the skin.
- **Tea bags** will cure puffy eyes in a jiffy. Dampen two tea bags with cool water. Lie down for 10 minutes with a tea bag over each eye.
- **Olive oil and sugar** will help soften very rough hands, feet, and elbows. Smooth olive oil over the affected area and scrub with sugar. Wash the oil and sugar off with mild soap and water.

Having a bad hair day?

Solve your problem with one of the following treatments.

- **For deep conditioning:** Work ½ cup of mayonnaise through wet hair. Wrap hair in a warm towel for 20 minutes and then shampoo as usual. You may need to shampoo twice.
- **For deep conditioning and shine:** Combine one mashed avocado and the juice of half a lemon to clean, damp hair. Work into hair and allow to sit for 10 minutes. Rinse with warm water until hair feels clean.
- **For shine and body:** Work two or three beaten egg whites into clean, damp hair. Wrap your hair in a towel and leave on for 10 minutes. Rinse thoroughly.
- **To remove build-up from styling products:** Wash your hair and rinse thoroughly with white vinegar.

If your area is home to many families with young children, you may want to organize a full-blown baby-sitting co-op (see the chart that follows). Once you have the children covered, you're free to plan a date. The question is, what are you going to do? An intimate dinner in a white-tablecloth restaurant probably won't fit into your budget every week, but here are some ideas.

Baby-sitting co-ops

Many parents find that a baby-sitting co-op is the perfect answer to the babysitter dilemma. In addition to free baby-sitting, such co-ops offer a chance to get to know other local families with small children. Ask around or call parents' groups in your area to find out if a baby-sitting co-op exists. If there's not a co-op in your neighborhood, consider starting one. Every baby-sitting co-op is set up to met the needs of its members, but they all work basically the same way:

♦ Baby-sitting co-ops may have a handful of families, or they may have as many as 50. The more families a co-op has, the more administration it requires.
♦ All co-ops have a set of rules by which all members must abide.
♦ Typically, members are added only after their home has been inspected for hazards. For example, a family who has a swimming pool with no fence may not be eligible for membership.
♦ Baby-sitting is exchanged among the members based on a point or ticket system. If someone watches your child, for example, it may cost you one point (or ticket) per hour per child. New members may be granted a small number of points when they join, and they earn more points by baby-sitting another member's children.
♦ Administrative duties often rotate among the members of the co-op. For example, a certain family may be responsible for keeping track of points, updating and mailing out telephone lists, and planning meetings for six months. Then it's someone else's turn.
♦ Co-ops often have social get-togethers periodically so members can get to know each other.
♦ Many co-ops charge members a small annual fee to cover postage and photocopying.

Go to an art gallery or two. Unlike museums, small galleries don't usually charge an entrance fee. Some museums also offer free admittance early in the week.

Go parking, grown-up style. No matter where you live you probably have some beautiful scenery or views within a short drive. Pack a light picnic and go catch a sunset or watch the moon come up.

Go out for coffee or dessert, or both. Have dinner at home with the kids and then head out to a coffeehouse. Or, if you feel like dressing up, reserve a table at a great restaurant for after-dinner drinks and dessert.

Go for a drive. It doesn't have to be a Sunday afternoon; just get in the car and go.

Go to a free concert. Many cities have a free outdoor concert series in the summer. Watch for details in the entertainment section of your local paper. Also consider checking out your local college, or art center, for free concerts.

Stop by a nightclub. These aren't all for the singles crowd only. Many areas have jazz or folk clubs that cater to a more mature (and sedate) clientele. You may have to pay a cover charge to get in.

Go to a movie. Second-run movie houses are becoming more common. You may be able to catch a six-month-old release for a couple of dollars per ticket.

Go window shopping. When the weather is nice, go window shopping in the evening. The streets in the business district are usually well-lit. You can stroll leisurely because the crowds are gone, and, because the stores probably aren't open, you won't have the opportunity to make impulse purchases.

A variation on this theme is curb shopping. Take a drive through an upscale neighborhood. You can "ooh" and "aah" at the mansions, and if you own a home, you can get landscaping and exterior design ideas in the process. If you hit the same neighborhoods during "Parade of Homes" week, you can look around on the inside, too.

Go on a date at home. If you can't get a sitter, or if you just don't want to go out, have a date at home. Put the kids in bed at a reasonable hour, and have a grown-up picnic on the living room floor. Light some candles, and spread a tablecloth or blanket on the carpet. Dine on your favorite no-cook luxury foods such as expensive cheese, gourmet crackers, fresh strawberries, and a bottle of good wine. Use the real wine glasses and the linen napkins. Nibble on your picnic fare while you watch a romantic movie.

What to do with the kids in tow

We know as well as anybody that you can't always get away alone, but that doesn't mean you can't socialize anyway. Plan things with other parents, and the children can play while you visit.

Host a coffee klatch. The idea of a coffee klatch may make you think of cups, saucers, and gossip, but years ago it served an important purpose. A coffee klatch gave housewives a chance to meet with other women who also spent most of their time running a household and raising children. For some of these women, the coffee klatch was the only thing that kept them from being isolated. Keep the tradition alive. Set up a semi-monthly get-together with your friends for some conversation over a cup of hot java while your children play.

Play dates at the park. Meet friends and their kids at the park. The kids can play and the adults can chat while keeping an eye on everybody.

Start a book club. If you like to read and know other parents who like to read, too, consider starting a book club for stay-at-home parents. You can hold informal meetings in members' homes, and have everyone bring the kids. Depending on the ages of the children, you may need to hire an older sibling as a sitter, or take turns watching the little ones.

Have a potluck luncheon. Every once in a while have a potluck luncheon. Call your friends and tell them that you'll make lunch for the kids, if they will bring food for the grown-ups.

Plan a field trip. While going to the zoo or science museum with your family can be enjoyable, it can be even more fun to bring a friend. Next time you take your children on a weekday outing, invite another at-home parent and kids to come along.

Not~So~Famous Last Words

"Perhaps the greatest social service that can be
rendered by anybody to the country and to
mankind is to bring up a family."
—George Bernard Shaw

If you're still reading at this point, chances are excellent that you've made the conversion to a single-income family, or will do so soon. Although the decision to have one parent quit work must be made as a couple, you've probably noticed that the bulk of this book has been addressed directly to you, the stay-at-home parent. And no matter how excited you've been to quit your job and stay home, as you've read, we're sure there have been times you've thought, "Is this what it's all about? I'm going to quit my job only to condemn myself to a life of chasing children and doing housework?" We want to respond to that question.

Most of us who are raising a family today came of age at a time when the women's movement was not only in full swing, but had made quite a bit of headway into the American psyche. By the time we were in high school and entering college, we took it for granted that a girl could—and should—become whatever she wanted, even if she wanted to be a doctor, a lawyer, a scientist, or enter any other traditionally male-dominated field. We didn't hope to receive equal pay for equal work, we expected it. This is good, and just as it should be. But somewhere along the line, the notion that women were just as capable as men got translated into the idea that traditional women's work (baking cookies, wiping runny noses, and taking care of a home) was demeaning at best and proof of subservience to men at worst. With this, the pendulum had swung too far, and a generation of women is in danger of completely missing the point.

The fact is, household chores are not, nor were they ever meant to be, an end unto themselves. They are merely things that must be taken care of in order to meet a greater goal: creating and maintaining a healthy and stable environment for the good of the family. Throughout history and across cultures, the lion's share of housework has fallen to women. This isn't because women have always been considered inferior, but because, thanks to biology, women are the logical candidates to maintain the hearth while raising the children. That's not to say that there haven't been entire eras characterized by a male chauvinistic viewpoint, because there have. But it is to say that there's nothing inherently demeaning about housework. Although it's true that the hand that rocks the cradle is the hand that washes the diapers, the same hand also touches—and to a large degree, directs—the lives of the entire family, makes the most indelible mark upon the children, lays the groundwork for a future generation, and thereby effects the course of history.

That's what has always been in it for you.

Mary Snyder and Malia McCawley Wyckoff
June, 1999

Continuing Education

You can find resources for the one-income family in a variety of places, from small local groups to national organizations, and from newsletters to best-selling books. The following is a list of additional sources of inspiration and information.

Books

Cooking

Complete Guide to Home Canning, Preserving and Freezing, revised edition. U.S. Department of Agriculture. Dover Publications, 1994.
This book contains the most up-to-date information of safely preserving food.

Feed Me! I'm Yours, revised and updated. Vicki Lansky. Meadowbook Press, 1994.
A terrific cookbook for new parents, with advice and instructions on cooking for babies and small children.

Frozen Assets: How to Cook for a Day and Eat for a Month. Deborah Taylor-Hough. Champion Press Ltd., 1998.
A simple and straightforward guide for cooking once a month. The book has a complete, step-by-step process to making and storing meals and also offers worksheets and tips for frugal shopping.

How to Cook Everything: Simple Recipes for Great Food. Mark Bittman. Macmillan General Reference, 1998.
A real "how-to" cookbook with more than 1,500 recipes.

Putting Food By, 4th new revised edition. Janet C. Greene, Ruth Hertzberg, and Beatrice Vaughn, contributor. Penguin USA, 1992.
The latest edition of the food preservation classic includes new information on freezing for the microwave, gifts, and canning convenience food.

The Fannie Farmer Cookbook, 13th revised edition. Marion Cunningham. Alfred A. Knopf, 1997.
The latest revision of the cookbook that's been teaching Americans how to cook for 100 years. This comprehensive cookbook includes illustrations, clear instructions, and helpful comments throughout.

The Freezer Cooking Manual. Nanci Slagle and Tara Wohlenhaus. Self-published (800-9-Manual).
This manual features a comprehensive, easy-to-follow system for assembling and freezing tasty and nutritious entrees, side dishes and snacks for up to six weeks at a time. The manual is full of tips and practical advice, tally sheets and over 60 recipes.

The New Joy of Cooking. Irma S. Rombauer, et al. Scribner, 1997.
An all-new update of the comprehensive classic. Contains approximately 3,000 recipes, explains cooking basics, and includes illustrations.

Home and family

American Academy of Pediatrics Guide to Your Child's Symptoms: The Official, Complete Home Reference, Birth Through Adolescence. The American Academy of Pediatrics, Donald Schiff and Seven P. Shelov, Editors. Villard Books, 1999.
The ultimate pediatric answer book.

How to Organize a Baby-sitting Cooperative & Get Some Free Time Away From the Kids. Carole T. Myers. Carousel Press, 1976.
Everything you need to know about setting up a baby-sitting co-op.

Joey Green's Encyclopedia of Offbeat Uses for Brand Name Products. Joey Green. Hyperion, 1998.
Joey Green, the author of *Paint Your House with Powdered Milk, Polish Your Furniture with Pantyhose,* and *Wash Your Hair with Whipped Cream,* reviews 120 name brand products, from Alka Seltzer to Ziploc storage bags, and offers alternate uses for all of them. A fun and humorous resource guide.

Not for Packrats Only: How to Clean Up, Clear Out, and Live Clutter-Free Forever. Don Aslett. New American Library, 1991.

The more junk you have, the more junk you have to deal with. Don Aslett will help you declutter permanently.

Reader's Digest New Complete Do-It-Yourself Manual. The Reader's Digest Association, 1991.

This is the updated version of the classic and comprehensive home-maintenance guide.

The Doctor's Book of Home Remedies. The editors of *Prevention* magazine. Bantam, 1991.

Thousands of doctor-approved home remedies.

The Mother's Almanac, revised edition. Marguerite Kelly & Ella Parsons. Doubleday, 1992.

The national bestseller, now updated and revised for the 90s. This book is loaded with practical advice and information.

365 TV-free Activities You Do With Your Kids, 2nd edition. Steven J. Bennett and Ruth Bennett. Adams Publishing, 1996.

A great book for helping parents get their kids away from the television. This guide is filled with easy activities that require few, if any, props and that get and hold the attention of children for hours.

Tiptionary. Mary Hunt. Broadman & Holman Publishers, 1997.

From the editor of *Cheapskate Monthly*, this book is filled with hundreds of valuable tips for family, home, food, cars, personal finance, and travel. It's a humorous and handy guide to making the most of your money and your time.

Lifestyle/philosophy

Simplify Your Life. Elaine St. James. Hyperion, 1994.

More than 100 ways to simplify everyday living so you can enjoy.

The Simple Life. Larry Roth. Berkley Publishing Group, 1998.

A book by a master of simple living, filled with contributions by many people in the simplicity/frugality movement. A hefty resource guide filled with hundreds of tips.

The Simple Living Guide. Janet Luhrs. Broadway Books, 1997.

Often called "the bible of the simplicity movement," this book covers every area your life that can be simplified. Even if you're not looking to become a practitioner of voluntary simplicity, this book has some wonderful and easy ideas for getting more enjoyment out of life.

Money

Bonnie's Household Budget Book: The Essential Workbook for Getting Control of Your Money. Bonnie Runyan McCullough. St. Martin's Press, 1996.

This guide helps readers to set up budgets and take control of daily finances, regardless of income level.

Invest in Yourself: Six Secrets to a Rich Life. Marc Eisenson, Gerri Detweiler, and Nancy Castleman. John Wiley & Sons, 1998.

Invest in Yourself offers a six-step process for readers to assess their wants and needs and lead them to create a richer, more fulfilling life. The book offers a mix of down-to-earth philosophy, financial strategies, and money-saving ideas.

The 9 Steps to Financial Freedom. Suze Orman. Crown Publishing, 1997.

Orman's financial advice is solid and workable. Even if you're put off by the New Age spiritual approach to personal finance, this book is still worth a read if only for the discussion of the emotional power that money and spending have on everyone.

The Millionaire Next Door: The Surprising Secrets of America's Wealthy. Thomas J. Stanley and William D. Danko. Longstreet Press, 1996.

Fascinating information about the people who *really* hold the wealth in the United States.

The Overspent American: Upscaling, Downshifting, and the New Consumer. Juliet B. Schor. Basic Books, 1998.

The author of *The Overworked American* analyzes America's spending habits.

Your Money or Your Life: Transforming Your Relationship With Money and Achieving Financial Independence. Joe Dominguez and Vicki Robin. Penguin USA, 1993.

Even if you don't follow the author's nine steps, this book will change the way you view your money and, therefore, spend it!

Newsletters

A Penny Saved
PO Box 3471
Omaha, NE 68103-0471
E-mail: apnnysvd@juno.com
Web site: www.mindspring.net/~apennysaved/index.html

$15/6 issues—Sample issue: $3
A Penny Saved is dedicated to helping people learn how to be thrifty (without being cheap) and how to live well (without going broke in the process).

Balancing Act
PO Box 309
Ghent, NY 12075-0309
E-mail: BalancingA@aol.com

$6.00/6 issues—Sample issue: $1 (send SASE)
Balancing Act promotes simple living using creative frugality. Each issue has tips on gardening, crafts, cooking, decorating, family fun, and more.

Counting the Cost
Suite 122
4770 Riverdale
Memphis, TN 38141
E-mail: counting.the.cost@excite.com
Web site: www.members.xoom.com/NancyT/CTChome.htm

$15/12 issues—Sample issue: $2
A newsletter for people practicing the art of simple and frugal living. It is for everyone who wants to get more out of life without going into debt doing it.

Creative Downscaling—Edith Kilgo, Editor
PO Box 1984
Jonesboro, GA 30237-1884
(770) 471-9048 (Tuesday through Thursday)
E-mail: Kilgo@mindspring.com
Web site: www.mindspring.com/~kilgo/index.html

$15/6 issues—Sample issue: $2
For a Resource Guide, send 55-cent stamp (not a SASE)
Creative Downscaling (formerly *Simple Living News*) focuses on those who want to downscale, de-stress, and simplify their lives.

You *Can* Afford to Stay Home With Your Kids

Frugal Family Network Newsletter
PO Box 92731, Dept. Y
Austin, TX 78709
(512) 891-9031
E-mail: frugal4u@frugalfamilynetwork.com
Web site: www.frugalfamilynetwork.com

$10/6 issues—Sample issue: send SASE legal envelope
This newsletter offers regular features such as "Cook's Corner," "Feature Recipe," "Smart Gift Ideas," and "Quick Tips." The editors are dedicated to sharing homemaking skills for those who wish to make their dollar go further.

Simple Living
4509 Interlake Ave. N #149
Seattle, WA 98103
(206) 464-4800
Web site: www.slnet.com/cip/slj/slj.htm

$16/4 issues
The Boston Globe called this quarterly journal "the nation's premier newsletter on voluntary simplification." It includes real-life stories of people who have created rich lives through slowing down, as well as articles and tips by experts in the field. *Simple Living* also provides a forum for readers to connect via study circles, pen pals, and letters to the editor.

The Dollar Stretcher
PO Box 23785
Ft. Lauderdale, FL 33307
E-mail: gary@stretcher.com
Web site: www.stretcher.com

$18.00/12 issues—Sample issue: $2
The Dollar Stretcher covers all areas of saving time and money on everything from your home and car to vacations.

The Frugal Gazette
PO Box 3395
Newtown, CT 06470
(888) 811-6439
E-mail: Cindy@frugalgazette.com
Web site: www.frugalgazette.com

$18.95/12 issues or $36.95/24 issues—Sample issue: Send a legal-size SASE. (If you mention that you read about *The Frugal Gazette* in this book, the subscription prices are $12/12 issues or $24/24 issues.)

The Frugal Gazette is a monthly newsletter dedicated to helping people reduce their living expenses. Thousands of people throughout the United States find motivation and support from the "Pied Piper of Frugality," Cindy McIntyre, as she shares her experience and knowledge in this monthly newsletter.

The Pocket Change Investor
Good Advice Press
PO Box 78
Elizaville, NY 12523
E-mail: goodadvice@ulster.net
Web site: www.goodadvicepress.com

$12.95/4 issues—Sample issue: $2
Learn the newest techniques to save on taxes, credit cards, closing costs, cars, insurance, appliances, utilities, vacations, trips to the supermarket, and a myriad of other expenses we all face.

The Parenting Pages
RD 1 Box 1150
Springvale, Maine 04083
E-mail: redmonds@concentric.net
Web site: www.concentric.net/~redmonds

$10/4 issues—Sample issue: $3 (This fee can be credited toward your subscription price if you order a subscription within two months of requesting a sample issue.)
A quarterly newsletter that covers education, manners, nutrition, couple time, play, toys, and topics of interest to all parents. The newsletter features common sense with a "can-do" attitude, rather than just relying on the experts.

Organizations

International MOMS Club (Moms Offering Moms Support)
25371 Rye Canyon Road
Valencia, CA 91355
E-mail: Momsclub@aol.com

When writing to the organization for information, please enclose $2 to cover costs. The response will include either a person to contact for local information or materials on how to start a club. MOMS Club represents more than 27,000 members and 700-plus local chapters across the country. They offer monthly meetings, playgroups, baby-sitting co-ops, and social activities for mothers with children of all ages.

You *Can* Afford to Stay Home With Your Kids

MOPS (Mothers of Preschoolers)
PO Box 10220
Denver, CO 80250-2200
Web site: www.MOPS.org

Approximately 2,000 MOPS groups meet in churches throughout the United States, Canada, and 11 other countries to address the needs of more than 80,000 women each year. The members are of many ages and backgrounds, but share the common goal to be the best mothers they can be. To find out if there is a MOPS group near you, or to access the media arms of MOPS, call 303-733-5353 or 800-929-1287. E-mail: Info@MOPS.org. To learn how to start a MOPS group call 1-888-910-6677.

Index